LITTLE PRISSY AND T.C.

By
Colene Copeland

Illustrated by
Edith Harrison

Jordan Valley Heritage House
Publisher

T. Whitcomb Elem.

Pig out on books!

Colene Copeland
1997

LITTLE PRISSY AND T.C.

Copyright 1988, by Colene Copeland

Manufactured in the U.S.A.
Library of Congress Catalog
Card number: 88-081916

ISBN: 0-938810-07-7 (Hardcover)
ISBN: 0-938810-08-5 (Paperback)

Revised Edition

Dedication

*There was one special teacher who seemed to know
the things I would need to know in my life.
These are the things she taught me.*

*Thank you Evelyn Miller.
This one's for you.*

Table of Contents

Chapter 1.

PRISSY HEARS A RUMOR

"**W**ould they really sell me to someone else?" Little Prissy asked herself. "Would they really, ---just because I remind them of Priscilla? How could they do that to me?"

Little Prissy knew full well that when Mama and Papa were around her, their thoughts were on Priscilla, her mother, who had been dead for several months. Seeing Prissy sometimes made Mama cry! Naturally, she felt sorry for Mama, but could Prissy help it if she reminded them of Priscilla? Was that her fault?

Prissy was sure that Mama and Papa loved her as much as, or more than, any other animal on the farm. She loved them, too. Perhaps their feeling for her was not as great as it had been for her mother, but, nevertheless, she was loved a lot and knew it!

"Why did my mother have to become so popular,

1

---so revered, before she died?" Little Prissy mused as she stared out the wide front door. It wasn't that she disliked her mother. Not at all! She loved Priscilla! But the problem was, so did everyone else! Not only did they love Priscilla, they adored her and never stopped talking about her kind, heroic deeds!

"Of course I'm proud of my mother and the things she did," Little Prissy thought. "If only the sows would think of me as me, 'Prissy', and not as 'Priscilla's daughter'."

"If only there was something I could do to make them think differently of me, something special, soul-stirring and exciting." Little Prissy's heartbeat quickened! Oh, how wonderful it would be to become really important to the other sows! To be noticed, maybe famous! A little famous would be nice, but a whole bunch of famous would be a heck of a lot better!

She thought about it for a long time, enjoying an unusually warm, happy feeling. But finally, the flutter of the moment took wings. Reality set in. Reality has a way of being cruel sometimes, especially today.

The little sow was sad, for she truly believed herself to be a nobody. Nothing short of a miracle could remove such unfounded thoughts from her mind. "Life is just one batch of slug slime in the hog trough after another," she told herself.

Now, there was a new set of painful facts to be considered. Rosie had overheard one of the younger sows telling Victoria that she had over-heard Mama and Papa discussing a matter most distressing! PRIS-SY MIGHT BE SOLD TO ANOTHER FARMER! Why? Because Papa and Mama, the owners of the farm, were having a difficult time adjusting to Priscilla's death. Little Prissy's presence, as Priscilla's only off-spring, tended to remind them, all too often, of the one they had loved more than any other animal on the farm. Priscilla! Of course!

Rosie could not wait to tell Prissy what she had heard! When bad news was entrusted to Rosie as the carrier pigeon, with the accent on "pig" -eon, *that* news moved as swiftly as the scent of cheap perfume in a speeding elevator!

Rosie had an unusual personality, for a hog. Actually, she appeared to have several! One day she was as pleasant as could be and as good as she looked. For she did look good, a perfectly formed, lovely white Yorkshire. Round where she should be round, and long and lean where she should be long and lean. The next day she might turn into a real hooligan, an honest-to-goodness desperado, terrorizing those who would allow it and bullying the younger, unsuspecting creatures in the farrowing barn.

But, all the sows agreed, Rosie would sometimes do one thing that they considered terrific. Periodically, the lovely little hellion would retire to a corner of her pen, and peace and quiet would reign. It was as if she sentenced herself to a day of solitary confinement, as if she were infectious! She did nothing but eat and sleep. Her peers were quite convinced that she set aside these days to conjure up more schemes with which to intimidate, torment and in general, disrupt their daily lives. This day of days had come to be known as, "Rid of Rosie Day"! A real holiday!

Rosie was a devilish sow, not at all like her mother, Rachel, or her twin sister, Posey. She fattened on gossip, and took great pleasure in putting the other sows in a bad light. Still, her greatest talent lay in turning a bad situation into a major, hopeless catastrophe. She would set her mouth in motion, and by the time Rosie finished, the ax had fallen, the war was lost and all were defeated except Rosie! By then, she had another notch on her pigskin holster! And, in her eyes only, had raised her status in life to a more prestigious height.

Now, she wallowed in immeasurable delight as she blurted out this cruel rumor to Prissy.

"They are going to sell you!" she announced, feasting on each word. "You remind them too much of your mother!" ---The shot was fired!

The announcement caught Little Prissy quite by surprise! She stumbled for words of denial. But they stuck in her throat. She feared the worst, ---Rosie was telling the truth. During the week that followed, Prissy thought of little else.

"Is the story true?" She had inquired of the other sows. One by one they admitted to her that they, too, had heard the same rumor.

Prissy tried not to think about it. She could ask Mama! But she knew she would never have the nerve. For if Mama and Papa had decided to sell her, they were looking for just the right farmer. And, there was not a thing she could do about it!

It was quite late when Prissy finally fell into a troubled sleep.

Chapter 2.

ONE SIDED CONVERSATIONS

Sometime in the night, Prissy had a curious dream about T.C. She dreamed he was alive and well, but lonely! In the dream, Tom Cat had long gray whiskers. Not the ordinary kind. These stuck out about a foot on each side of his head. They looked pretty silly. At one point in the dream, the cat did a headstand. The whiskers were so strong that they kept him from falling over! When Prissy awoke, the dream was so real that she looked up to the rafters, T.C.'s favorite perch, half expecting to see him there.

"No wonder I dream crazy dreams about that cat," Prissy thought. "That's the way I remember him, always doing the unexpected, ---full of surprises! But always, he was a trusted friend to my mother and to me. I didn't even mind when he called me his 'Little Porker'," she mused.

6

T.C. balancing on strong whiskers.

But the fun-loving Tom Cat had a tender heart. Priscilla's death had been too much for him. Soon after her death, he disappeared and had not been seen nor heard about, since.

"I do wish he would come home," Prissy thought,

as she remembered his keen talent for sleuthing. "He could nose around and report back to me. I'll bet he could find out what's going on in Papa's and Mama's heads."

Prissy watched as an old one-eyed cat skipped cautiously over the hot gravel in front of the barn. This summer had been unusually hot! The dry field corn bowed to the ground. Uninvited snakes became brave and turned up in unexpected places.

A torrid breeze blew little whirlwinds of dust through the cracks at each side of the window on the back wall of Prissy's pen. It whined a dismal tune.

Loneliness lay claim to Prissy's soul. The little sow needed someone, ---anyone, to talk to. Some friendly conversation would be nice. She surveyed neighboring sows within talking distance.

The farrowing barn was made up of pens, 10' square. Each sow had her own private space. Two rows of pens connected end to end, and were divided by a wide hallway. The building was all wood. Papa would never have his sows on cement!

There were only a few sows within the sound of her voice. She could shout. But, that would be rude! Her mother had taught her that shouting was not polite. So, the prospects for conversation were not good.

To her right, Elsie resided in the pen that once was Priscilla's. Prissy had been given the second pen, to be near her mother.

It was hard to believe now that Elsie was the bully who had made life miserable for Priscilla! They were sisters. Elsie had been jealous of Priscilla's life in the farm house, her vacations with the family and the special attention from Mrs. "C" (Mama). But before her death, Priscilla had captured Elsie's love and friendship, just as she had all the rest.

Prissy looked at Elsie and pondered a moment or two. Then she turned her attention to the left, to Victoria, one of the older sows. Victoria was a long white Yorkshire. Perhaps it was her age that made her so cranky. Perhaps not! At any rate, as she got older her crankiness picked up speed while Victoria herself, slowed down.

Despite her cantankerous manner, Victoria was a fine mother. Her pigs were always fat and happy. Nursing fourteen pigs this time had been a hectic experience for the poor old sow. By the time the pigs were five weeks old they were so strong and competitive they shoved their mother from one side of the pen to the other. But did Victoria complain? No! She did not! Not one peep!

Like many of the other sows, Victoria gave great oratories about Priscilla. She would rattle on and on about Priscilla's fantastic stories and extreme bravery. Prissy was definitely not in the mood for that kind of conversation!

Earlier in the day while Prissy was trying to rest on her straw, she could hear Victoria telling it again.

"When Priscilla became an adult and was moved into the farrowing barn she brought with her, kindness, politeness, gentleness, good manners and quiet eating habits. She taught us a few things, all right! She could have been spoiled, but she wasn't. For she had been raised in the farm house where Mr. and Mrs. "C" live. She was allowed to watch television, taken on vacation trips, and had the luxury of bubble baths in a big bathing tub. ---And then, there was that unforgettable night." Victoria paused, recalling quite vividly the horror of the experience. "Hotsie's death! ---and the way Priscilla jumped that high fence in the middle of the night to care for Hotsie's pigs!" Her voice was soft and tearful as she told the story to her children.

Prissy had heard it all many, many times. She, too, remembered all those things and more. There was no getting away from Priscilla's perfection.

Elsie would be the best bet for conversation. Most of the time, Elsie talked about vegetables.

Elsie had done what all the sows liked to do on a hot day. She had scratched the cedar shaving away, making a clear spot. Then she had overturned her water tub to make a cooler place to lie down. A right smart idea!

"Elsie," Little Prissy called through the 2x4's that

divided their pens. "What are you thinking about?"

"Prunes," she answered.

"What?" Prissy was surprised.

"I'm thinking about prunes!"

"Prunes aren't vegetables!" Prissy laughed.

"Never said they were, did I?"

"No, but you usually talk about vegetables!" Prissy said.

"My dear," Elsie groaned as if in great pain, "usually, I don't talk to you at all, ---about anything!"

"I know. But I listen when you talk to the other sows," Little Prissy replied sweetly.

"Well, don't!" Elsie snapped, and deliberately turned her back to a sad Little Prissy. Prissy had no idea what she had done to upset Elsie.

"I didn't mean to make you mad, Elsie," Prissy told her. But there was no reply.

Although hogs know how foods taste, they don't know fruits from vegetables, or for that matter, care. Rather than admit her ignorance to Prissy, Elsie had turned her back to shut Prissy out. Elsie had been outdone by a younger sow.

Prissy was not aware that her superior knowledge bothered her peers, although she knew she was constantly shunned. But why, she did not know. The sows weren't exactly cruel to Prissy; they just kept their distance and worked hard at not becoming too friendly with her, to avoid any embarrassment to themselves.

Prissy still wanted to talk to somebody. Maybe Peaches, she thought. Weren't our mothers best of friends? Hadn't Peaches' mother, Hotsie, been regarded highly, just as my mother was? With so much in common, Prissy wondered why the sows tolerated Peaches and would not tolerate her.

Peaches stood in her pen across the hall and scratched her hind side on the rough wooden wall.

"When are your pigs due to be born, Peaches?" Prissy asked. There was no answer.

"Peaches," she called again. The sow looked up but did not answer.

Prissy persisted. "When are your pigs due to arrive?"

"I don't keep track!" Peaches finally answered, reluctantly.

"When Mama comes, why don't I ask her for you?" Little Prissy offered, trying to be helpful.

"You don't have to call Mrs. "C" Mama, just because Priscilla did!" Rosie blurted, from across the hall. "After all, Priscilla was the one she raised in the house, not you!"

"But I got into the habit of calling her Mama when my mother was alive. Now, ---it just seems like the thing to do."

"Don't bother to ask her when my pigs are due to be born," Peaches added. "Not for me, anyway.

When they come, they come! Who cares about the date?"

"What's the use? I'm wasting my time," Prissy told herself, as she slowly turned around to lie down. "I might as well go stick my head in the rain barrel and end it all." In a barn full of hogs, Little Prissy felt sad and alone.

Prissy had done it again. She had intimidated another sow. This time it was Peaches. Peaches knew nothing of calendars and dates, and didn't care. As usual, Prissy had no notion of what crime she had committed.

Prissy truly had her problems. She wished again for T.C. Why doesn't he come home?

Chapter 3.

PISTON

Piston was an adopted burro, having been trucked in from Nevada range land two years ago. When grass became scarce, the wild burros began to be a nuisance to the ranchers. A government program was developed to save the animals and protect the ranchers. It was through that program that Glenn and Alice Greystone, nearby neighbors, adopted two of the little troublemakers. Piston and Stinger found a good home.

Stinger was satisfied to stay in the pasture to graze and snooze. But Piston was never satisfied. Piston went over, under and through gates and fences. Then he would stand and bray about it for half an hour, sometimes, half a day, just to say, "Look what I did, again!"

This burro had seen more of the Williamette Valley than anyone else. He had eaten from every vegetable garden and orchard in the area. Mr. Folger peppered him with his trusty BB gun. Mrs. Folger hated the beast!

One March night Piston kicked down the door of Mrs. Folger's brooder house containing 800 new born chicks. This particular night it was raining hard and a strong wind was blowing. The heavy rain blew right in the brooder house. By morning, when Mrs. Folger made her early visit to check on the baby chicks, the damage had been done. Only 120 of the tiny birds were alive, and out of the 120, only 47 lived. Piston was still in their yard, standing under a large pine.

Greystones were embarrassed and sorry. Mr. Greystone gave Mrs. Folger a check to cover all the damages. Mrs. Folger offered to shoot Piston, no charge! Mr. Folger suggested tying the cussed animal to the railroad tracks.

The Greystones became more embarrassed. They promised to tie Piston to a big tree until they could build a taller, stronger fence and hang an iron gate.

Now, guess who just walked through the front door of the farrowing barn? You guessed it! Piston! He was loose again!

"Better get outta here, Jack!" Victoria told him.

Piston cocked his head to one side. "No way! And, the name's not Jack!"

"All you donkeys are Jacks!" Rosie announced.

"And you are a dumb, slop-slurper!" Piston

There stood Piston in the barn doorway!

replied.

"Boy burros are Jacks and girl burros are Jen-
nys," Prissy said. "Piston is the name Glenn Grey-

stone gave him."

"Well, who ---, asked ---you?" Rosie inquired bit-
terly!

Piston laughed. He smiled at Prissy. Prissy knew
the mischievous little burro always made trouble, but
she couldn't help liking him. Listening to his wise-
cracks reminded her of T.C. as she thought once again
how much she missed him.

The visitor sauntered leisurely down the hallway.
Halfway back, he kicked open a bale of straw bedding, flopped down on it, and went to sleep.

One after the other shouts of suggestions were
given to Piston.

"Better get out while you have a chance!"

"Go home before you get caught!"

"You're in big trouble again, donkey!"

But Piston either didn't hear or didn't care about
what they said. When Papa came to feed and water,
he saw the uninvited guest. Quickly, he closed the
front door and went around the outside to close the
back so the animal would not escape.

Papa put a rope around Piston's neck and tied
him out under an apple tree. Piston seemed to enjoy
all the trouble he caused! Papa opened the doors so
the air could circulate through the barn.

Everybody knew they had not seen the last of
Piston.

Chapter 4.

CHANGES

The next day started off great for Prissy. A welcome change. Quickly, she popped up from her bed, tidied up her straw and drank for a few minutes at her water tub. She could see Mama and Papa hurring around in the barn. The barn doors, the big one up front and the one to the rear, had been shut. Little Prissy knew what was coming next. Hogs were going to be shifted around in the building. Then some would be moved out and others moved in. The doors were closed so no one could escape. There would be a great deal of action today.

Prissy had never been moved. What would it be like, she wondered? Papa had let her run around in the apple orchard several times, and every now and then she was allowed to run up and down the hallway. But always, she returned to the same pen, the second one from the door. It was home. Long ago,

18

Victoria darted out! Papa jumped aside!

Mama had promised Prissy that she would never be moved. But things are different now, she thought.

The minute her gate was opened, Victoria wasted no time darting out. Papa jumped aside to avoid being run over by the delighted old sow. It was her turn to roam up and down the hallway. She chatted happily with old friends, completely ignoring the younger sows. They probably didn't care, anyway.

Victoria's day had come. She would be turned out to pasture for a nice long rest. Cool resting spots, shaded by great Oregon pine trees, awaited her. How splended!

Then Elsie was moved, leaving the front pen vacant.

Papa and Mama worked fast to complete the moving before the hot sun cooked up nasty tempers here in hog city.

As the morning advanced, hot dang, Prissy smiled, things just got better. Mama opened the gate to Elsie's empty pen. Seeming very pleased, an old Landrace sow limped in.

Prissy was ecstatic. She whirled around in her pen scattering cedar shavings. Some flew into her drinking water.

"Mabel!" Prissy greeted the old sow happily. Now, there would be someone to talk to. "How good to have you for a neighbor!"

Mabel drank from the water tub for several minutes.

"You see! *She* doesn't want to talk to you either!" Peaches snapped, from across the hall.

"That's what you think," Mabel answered hastily, giving the sow a defiant little smile.

Prissy was delighted.

"All that walking tires me out, Prissy," Mabel

said. "Makes me thirsty too!"

Peaches turned her back to pout. Prissy had had a victorious moment. She enjoyed it! Then she turned her attention back to the old sow, looking her over thoroughly.

"Don't tell me you are going to have another litter of pigs?" Prissy asked her.

Mabel looked surprised by the question!

"You should be retired!" Prissy persisted.

"Retired? What does that mean? I declare, Prissy, you are just like your mother, always using words that the rest of us don't understand!" Mabel, at least, admitted it.

"I'm sorry, Grandmother." Prissy said shyly. "You are right, of course. I did learn a lot from my mother. She said when 'people' get old, they retire. They go fishing, take vacations or plant a little garden. Then they sit on the back porch and watch it grow."

"But my dear Little Prissy," Mabel exclaimed, "I am not 'people'! I'm a hog! Going fishing and planting a little garden are not on my list of things to do."

"Oh, I know that! All I'm saying is, I think it's time you rest. You could enjoy the pasture, ---just eat and sleep," Prissy insisted.

"I do appreciate you, child, the way you care about my welfare. That's real nice. But there seems to be some things you don't know about me. I love having babies around me. They come and they go. After a while I get to wishing for more." Mabel looked thoughtfully at Prissy. "Being put out to pasture sounds, ---real, ---boring."

"But Mabel," Prissy persisted. "Pigs are pesky. A half a dozen of them are always under my belly when I want to lie down! One or two want to nurse when I want to sleep! You have to admit, that's pretty pesky! There's more! A couple of them are always fighting, chewing on each other's ears. They squeal and kick up the dust. They play in the drinking water and overturn the tub. But the thing I dislike most, the very peskiest, the minute I lie down, one of them always wants to take a nap, ---on my head! You can't deny it, Mabel! Pigs are pesky!"

Mabel did not respond. Perhaps she had not heard a word. The tired old sow had gone to sleep.

Prissy had been so preoccupied with the joy of having Mabel near that for the moment, at least, she had forgotten her troubles.

With Mabel asleep, once again Prissy's mind returned to the thing that caused her to worry. When the time was right and nobody was listening, she would ask Mabel about the rumor. Mabel would not lie to her. Prissy wondered if she really wanted to hear the truth. Maybe it was better not to know.

The poor little sow lay motionless on the floor and in secret, cried herself to sleep.

Chapter 5.

THE SECRET

Christina and Sara were Mama's and Papa's granddaughters. They loved to visit and explore the farm. Prissy could hear them talking as they ran through the orchard headed for the farrowing barn. When they reached the door they began saying "hello" to all the hogs. In fact, the two of them ran down the hallway, "helloing" each sow, one after the other!

"Hello hog," Christina would say.

"Hello hog," Sara repeated, until each and every hog had been thoroughly greeted. Then out the back door they ran, heading back across the apple orchard.

Later they were poking around in the chicken house when they spied several hens sitting on hatching eggs.

"I want to see one of them hatching eggs," Sara demanded!

The hens did not trust Sara.

"*Those,* Sara! And you'd better not bother around the setting hens. They'll peck you! And if Grandpa and Grandma find out, they'll be mad!" Christina told her.

"But I want to see a hatching egg," Sara insisted.

"Come on, Sara! Let's get out of here before you get us in trouble!" Christina said, as she walked out of the chicken house, leaving Sara behind.

Sara kept looking at the setting hens. The hens were watching Sara with a great deal of distrust. Temptation was too great! Sara crept nearer the hens and peeked over into one of the nesting boxes. The hen, a large Plymouth Rock, lifted herself somewhat, making loud clucking noises and spreading her wings. Sara didn't dare touch the eggs, but she could see some of them. How surprised she was to learn that the hatching eggs looked exactly like every other egg she'd ever seen. Disappointed, she turned and stomped out the door.

Meanwhile, Christina was exploring near the pine trees by the duck pond. She had grown fond of Shuffles, Papa's old duck. But where was Shuffles? This time of day, she was always on the pond, or near it.

"Let's play hide and seek, Christy," Sara shouted from behind a giant pine tree.

Christina did not answer. She was too busy searching for Shuffles.

Papa came out the back door of the house and saw the girls down by the pond. He didn't know that Christina was looking for Shuffles, but he did know the girls were getting too close. Close enough to make him worry! Papa figured he'd better go down to the pond and protect his duck.

The girls saw him coming.

"Where's Shuffles, Grandpa?" Christina hollered. "I can't find her anywhere!"

"That's what I've come to show you," he answered.

Taking the girls by the hands, he walked up the bank to a small three-sided shed. Papa's head almost

Up popped Shuffles!

touched the roof. He lead the girls inside.

"Be quiet now and I'll show you something," Papa told them.

There was a bale of wheat straw laying catty-cornered at the back of the shed. Up from behind it popped the head of a duck!

"What's Shuffles doing back there, Grandpa? What's she hiding for?" Sara asked.

"She isn't hiding, Sara," Papa smiled. "She's sitting on hatching eggs. In about three days they'll begin hatching. Now don't bother around the shed,

girls. We don't want to disturb Shuffles and cause her
to break her eggs or to leave her nest."

"What about the hatching hens, Grandpa? When
will their eggs hatch?" Sara asked.

Papa laughed. "I think you mean 'setting hens',
Sara. I'm not sure about the hens. Grandma takes
care of that. You ask her. It's marked on the calendar
in the kitchen."

Sara ran for the house.

"Sara sure is interested in those setting hens,"
Christina confided to her grandpa.

"She likes chickens and you like ducks. Am I
right, Christina?" Papa asked.

"Right, Grandpa," she smiled. Papa left for the
farrowing barn.

Christina stood outside the shed for a long moment and watched Shuffles. Mindful of grandpa's instructions not to disturb the duck, she left quietly. As
she skipped down to the pond, she tried to picture in
her mind what it would be like when Shuffles took
her baby ducks into the water. She wondered how
many eggs were in the nest. Would they all hatch?
Would they all be white, like Shuffles? Would they all
be the same size? Was there such a thing as a "runt
duck"? Christina remembered what her grandmother
had told her about Priscilla. Priscilla had been grandma's favorite pig, she thought, and *that* pig was a
runt. There was a big picture of Priscilla hanging in
the house.

That evening, at the supper table, Christina and Sara chattered non-stop. Papa and Mama were happy because the girls were enjoying their visit.

"Don't them old hens get tired sittin' on them eggs all the time, Grandma? Don't they ever get up and walk around?" Sara asked.

"I think they're too busy to think about getting tired, Sara. The setting hens have to turn their eggs two or three times a day, and they have to stay on them to keep them just the right temperature, so they will hatch," Mama explained. "But they do get off the nest. I put feed in the chicken yard every morning, early. They get off long enough to eat. I suppose that takes them about 30 minutes or so."

The girls were excited to learn that the eggs under Shuffles and those under the old Plymouth Rock, the hen whose eggs Sara had peeked at, would hatch the same day.

Christina and Sara bathed early and went to bed in the guest room. They were tired, but not too tired to talk and giggle and come up with a *secret plan.* Tomorrow, they would carry out their plan. For tomorrow evening they had to go home.

Early the next morning the girls were up and out of the house. Sara headed one way and Christina the other. A few minutes later they had their heads together, laughing. Mission accomplished!

What had they done? What was their Secret Plan?

The last thing they did before getting into the car to go home was to make a farewell tour through the farrowing barn.

"Goodbye hog," Christina shouted.

"Goodbye hog," Sara echoed, as they said their goodbyes to each animal in the barn.

"We'll be back, everybody," Christina announced to the apple trees as they raced to the car.

Would their secret be safe until they returned?

Chapter 6.

THE SURPRISE

Papa came in from the farrowing barn.

"Something's wrong with Little Prissy, Mama. You had better have a look at her. I don't think she's sick, ---I don't think," he repeated thoughtfully.

"Well, what do you think is the matter with her?" Mama asked.

"Danged if I know! You find out. She talks to you!" Papa laughed. Papa always liked to tease Mama, yet he had never been able to figure out how she could carry on a conversation with Priscilla and now with Little Prissy, while he could not.

"I thought she'd be better satisfied when we put Mabel next to her," Mama said. "I'll go check on her, after a bit."

The phone rang. It was Deana, Mama's and Papa's daughter.

"The girls are anxious to know if any of the eggs have hatched," she said.

"I don't know. I haven't looked yet." Mama answered.

"I've never seen Christina and Sara so anxious and so secretive about anything! By the way, the girls have named your old Plymouth Rock hen. They call her 'Scrambled Eggs'. Each time they say her name, they giggle. I guess it is a pretty funny name for a chicken."

"You tell the girls, as soon as the eggs are all hatched, I'll call you back. O.K.?" Mama asked.

"O.K." Deana answered.

Mama was in no hurry to check the hatching eggs. She knew the birds should have peace and quiet while the hatching is going on, otherwise there could be problems. Anyway, she wanted to go see what was bothering Prissy.

Prissy was happy when Mama walked through her gate. Some of the sows disapproved when Prissy would visit with Mama, obviously jealous. But, Prissy didn't care; she liked the company. After all, the little sow had always believed that Mama liked her better than all the others. Could she have been mistaken?

Mama sat down on Prissy's straw, pulled an apple from her apron pocket and handed it to her friend.

"I've been neglecting you, Prissy." Mama said. "Sorry! I promise I'll do better."

"I'm not sick or anything. But I sure get lonesome."

"I guess you've been busy." Prissy replied.

"Pretty busy. Had fun with my granddaughters when they were here. Are you feeling all right, Prissy?"

"I'm not sick or anything. But I sure get lonesome."

"Lonesome?" Mama questioned.

"I'll tell you something, Mama," she whispered. "Other hogs don't seem to get lonely. They are satisfied with just food and lodging. But not me! I like conversation!"

Mama laughed, keenly aware of just how much

like Priscilla she was. "How about Mabel? Why don't you talk to her?"

"She's O.K., I like her a lot, but brother, can she ever sleep!"

"You need Tom Cat, Prissy. He's the one that kept your mother entertained," Mama sympathized.

"But he's not here and he's never gonna be here," the little sow insisted.

"I hope you're wrong," Mama smiled, "I hope one day he struts through that door and makes us all laugh, just as he always did."

"Eggs are hatching today, Prissy. More ducks and chickens. In a few days, they'll be marching right through here."

Prissy did not answer. There was a question on the tip of her tongue. But she could not ask it. It was time for Mama to go, but she promised she would drop in again that evening.

Mama's day proved to be a busy one. Nothing unusual about eggs hatching; it did not demand her attention. She completely forgot about her Plymouth Rock until late afternoon, when it was time to gather the eggs from the laying hens. When she opened the chicken house door, the sweet music of peeping chicks greeted her ears. "Scrambled Eggs" was clucking to her babies and the babies were cheeping in answer. It was happy talk. After all, it can't be too much fun being cooped up in an egg shell.

Mama did not disturb the hen. She had been tending 18 eggs for three weeks. Now the eggs had turned into little golden peepers. The nesting box was full. All the eggs had hatched.

When Mama turned to leave, she thought she heard a strange sound coming from the nest. No, it couldn't be, she thought. It's just my imagination!

At supper, Papa and Mama agreed they would put the new family on the ground the next day! Later that evening, after they had visited Little Prissy, they returned to check on the Plymouth Rock. Papa lifted up the hen to throw out the empty shells.

"What's this?" he asked. There among the chicks, looking as out of place as a dirty sock on the dinner table, sat a little baby duck.

"That explains the big egg shell," he said. "Look Mama! How did it happen?" They stared at each other for a moment, and then set out for the three-sided shed. Papa raised up the duck. Sure enough! This time it wasn't such a big surprise! Among the baby ducks, sat a wee baby chick, the smallest of the lot.

"Those girls! This is what they've been giggling about! They switched eggs!" Papa laughed.

"Now what? Shall we switch them back?" Mama asked.

"Not yet! Let them have their fun!" Papa smiled.

Mama went to the house to call Deana. They had

a good laugh! Christina and Sara were relieved to find out their grandparents weren't too upset.

The next afternoon Deana brought the girls out to the farm. They wasted no time in getting out of the car. Sara ran to the chicken house and Christina to the three-sided shed. The nests were empty.

"What have you done with them, Grandpa?" Christina asked.

"I haven't done anything with them! They're running around here someplace," he told her.

"Let's go look, Christy!" Sara was excited. Off they ran.

Everybody searched. The duck and the hen, with their families, had been put on the ground early that morning. They had the run of the whole place and could be anywhere.

Maggie, the springer spaniel, began to bark. It was her "I've found them" bark. She was down by the pond. What a sight to see. Shuffles was in the water. One by one her babies were venturing in. All except one. The poor little chicken. It ran along the bank flapping it's wings, wondering what to do. It looked so pitiful.

Christina and Sara looked long and hard at the poor little chick. The smiles left their faces.

"I think we made a big mistake, Sara," Christina said sadly. Sara agreed.

"Looks to me like you girls have two choices,"

their mother told them. "You can teach that chicken to swim, or give it back to its mother."

With that bit of wisdom, Deana, Mama and Papa were just about to go away and let the girls figure it out, when Scrambled Eggs and her brood came into view. Then something happened that none of the group would ever forget.

Shuffles waddled out of the pond, calling to her ducklings and the baby chick. Around the chicken house came Scrambed Eggs, clucking to her chicks and the baby duck. The two families met and passed each other, face to face, both mothers calling to their young. The two little strangers heard their natural mother's voices. The hen headed to the right with *all* the baby chicks. Shuffles and *all* the ducklings quacked happily across the rose garden and into the orchard. It was a natural exchange, almost undetected!

Christina's and Sara's little prank had a happy ending. They had had their fun. They raced off to the farrowing barn to "hello" the hogs.

"I hope they don't try switching baby pigs," Papa chuckled. "That could cause real big trouble."

Chapter 7.

SPECIAL TREATMENT

gentle rain fell during the night. By morning, the grateful earth gave off a sweet fresh aroma.

Two sows had farrowed after midnight. Urma, Mabel's sister, had 15 pigs. One was born dead. The 14 were large and healthy looking. Six were white, like Mabel; three were black, and five were black with white belts around their middle, like Charlie, their father.

Peaches also farrowed. For the first time, the sow had a difficult delivery. The first three pigs came quickly. Pigs are born wide-eyed and walking! An hour and a half later, the fourth pig was born, --- after a little assistance from Papa. After number four, there were nine more, born in the next 45 minutes.

As soon as a pig was born Papa and Mama gave it a bath and put it under the heat lamp in the corner of the pen, away from the mother. When the pig was dry, Papa picked it up and using a pair of pointed pliers, clipped the sharp ends from the needle teeth. Pigs are born with several dark fangs, called needle teeth. If these teeth are not clipped, they can cause a great deal of damage and pain to the mother, when the pigs are nursing. Papa didn't want his sows damaged. The pigs squeal sometimes. But the dental work doesn't hurt them at all.

As soon as all her babies are born, Papa throws in fresh bedding for the sow. She gets up and rearranges the straw. When she's ready, she lies down and calls her family. They come running! The competition begins. The stronger pigs claim the best nursing spots. The weaker pigs are always shoved to the back nipples that contain less milk.

All the sows except Urma and Peaches had a cool night's rest. Even Prissy slept! Normally, she didn't sleep when Papa and Mama were in the barn at night. But the night was a great one for sleeping. The gentle rain made pleasant pattering sounds on the metal roof, making it difficult for Papa and Mama to keep their eyes open. There was very little sleep for them this night or any other night when pigs are being born.

After a couple of hours rest, they were back in the barn, doing chores and checking the new babies. All was well.

"You missed all the excitement last night, Prissy," Mama said, as she opened the gate. "Two new litters." Mama reached down, outside the gate, to pick up an armful of fresh straw for Prissy's pen. Suddenly, from the heart of the bundle, jumped a frightened, over-weight, gray mouse. It bleeped short, high-pitched sounds. The poor, pitiful creature ran to the edge of the pen, searching frantically for escape. There was none. Little Prissy paid no attention to it. But alas, an enemy heard the cry. There was an ear trained to listen for such sounds. A wild-eyed barn cat shot up to the top boards of the pen. With one pounce, the poor mouse was caught and killed. The cat leaped back to the top boards, strutting along, her catch dangling from her teeth.

The barn mice become plump from grain particles left by the hogs. The cats get fat on the mice. And so it goes, year after year.

"Mama, could I walk around outside with you for a while?" Prissy asked.

"Well, I'm not going to be doing much walking around, Prissy. I'm tired! Papa and I were up all night. But I guess we could take a little walk through the orchard." Mama opened Prissy's gate. The happy little sow stepped out. She trotted out the door and on to the orchard, but stopped quickly to munch on some fallen apples.

"Now I know why you wanted out, Prissy,"

Mama laughed, as she watched the sow "pig out" on apples.

Back in the farrowing barn, something was going on.

"Have you noticed how Priscilla's daughter always gets special treatment?" Rosie asked, with her front feet planted firmly on the top boards of her pen. "Mrs. 'C' is just buttering her up before they sell her!" Rosie announced.

"You don't know that for sure, Rosie!" Charlie spoke up. "If it's true, I'll hate to see her go. She's all that's left of Priscilla!"

"Not really!" Mabel replied. "There's *me*! And then there is Patsy and all of Prissy's other pigs!"

"I didn't mean to slight you, Mabel," Charlie said. "It's just that Prissy is Priscilla's only offspring."

"She'd better not come back in here today bragging about being 'taken for a walk'," Rosie piped.

"She would never do that, Rosie. It's just not her nature!" Mabel replied.

Too much of the time, the sows talked to each other as if Prissy didn't even exist. At least this time she couldn't hear Rosie's harsh words.

Mama and Prissy walked on through the orchard to the big machine shed which Priscilla and her good friend, Hotsie, had once called home. Now, the nice big pen inside was empty.

"I'm thinking of putting Patsy in here. I'd like to

keep this pen in the family, so to speak," Mama chuckled.

"How about *me* and Patsy?" Prissy asked.

"Well, we'll have to see," Mama answered.

I know what she'll have to see! She has to see if she's going to get rid of me or not, Prissy thought.

"Let's get you back, Prissy. I've got to go take a nap." As they walked back through the orchard, Mama thought of the times she had made this trip with Priscilla, Hotsie and that runaway Tom Cat. Whatever happened to T.C.?

Chapter 8.

A CHASE AND A STRANGE VISIT

T.C., that's short for Tom Cat, was the first friend Priscilla made after moving out of the house. And, when Little Prissy was born, T.C. would volunteer to piggy-sit while Priscilla slept. The problem was, T.C. would snuggle up with Little Prissy and fall sound asleep, himself! T.C. loved Little Prissy because she was smart, and good, and because she belonged to Priscilla. Priscilla's death caused him grief. But this proud, very cool cat would never let it show. Instead, the night Priscilla died, he hid, high in the rafters. The next morning, before anyone woke up, the heavy-hearted cat hit the road. He had no plans. Maybe he would return someday, maybe not!

Mama put ads in the local papers hoping to find him. Papa put a sign in the front yard. They asked around, but no one had seen T.C. Months passed. Only his closest friends still believed he might return.

T.C. first heard about the sandy beaches of southern California from Priscilla. She had been there with Mama and Papa on vacation and had told him of the sun and the sand.

Now, look who's on the beach! The Tom Cat himself, curled up by a friendly lady, in the shade of her beach umbrella. His eye was on the second half of her tuna fish sandwich. He knew precisely how to con a pretty lady. He had done it before, and it always worked. He stretched, purring prettily, and rubbed his head against her hand.

"Such a nice cat," the lady smiled.

Can you beat that? Not only did he get the sandwich, but some cold milk from a big green thermos. When his belly was full, he skillfully ske-daddled, before this kindly lady got ideas about taking him home for a nice little house pet. Wrong! No one would ever cage this crafty cat.

He darted around sun bathers, volley ball games, beach ball games, sand castles and teenage smoochers. Now and then some friendly soul would call to him. Some tried to snare him with food. But nothing would detain him now. His mind was made up. He was headed south again, to Redondo Beach! He'd hang around the pier. A cat's heaven! Fish. That was his reason for going. There were dozens of lazy fishermen who sat around in brightly colored yacht chairs, swapping stories. Some of them slept! But

A cat's heaven! Fish.

each of them had a line in the water. Live minnows baited the hooks. Each fisherman had fresh fish just lying there in his bucket. Handouts were often and deliciously generous. Some of the fishermen weren't interested in their catch, just the sport. Tom Cat made friends with *them* right away!

When the squalls hit the coast the cat still came away from the pier with a full stomach. After all, the pier is lined with fish shanties, each has a kitchen with a back door. People work in kitchens! There's bound to be a cat lover in the lot. Yes, he'd definitely head for Redondo Beach Pier.

Once off the sandy beach, Tom Cat made his way skillfully through a couple of back yards, just to pester a poodle and tease a terrier. He crossed a school yard and was about half way through a city park when he first laid eyes upon it! How wonderful! Terrific! Something to chase! How long had it been since he had had the sheer pleasure of a chase? And just for the heck of it!

The unsuspecting creature was a quick and cunning gray squirrel. The squirrel sat on her hind side nibbling her front feet, as if they itched! She gazed at the cat who now sat in a crouched position, body lowered and limbs bent. To the cat, it was all a lark!

He lunged toward the creature hoping to land squarely beside it, just to spook it a little. To harm the squirrel was not his intention. But, no one told that to the squirrel!

The startled little victim scampered around a large maple tree, over a picnic table and up a tall oak. So did the cat! Knowing he could catch the squirrel caused T.C. to produce an enormous grin, the likes of which this squirrel had never seen and the likes of which he hadn't worn for a long time. He careened in and out. It was his intention to stay a few feet behind, ---he wanted only to romp! But, how was the frightened little squirrel to know?

The chase continued. The squirrel tried all of her trusted escape routes, but she could not get rid of this cat!

Finally, she remembered her perfect escape spot. There was a hole in a high fence, several blocks away, large enough for her and too small for the grinning speed demon that followed close behind.

Off she ran, with Tom Cat hot on her heels. Now to add to his intimidation, T.C. let his tongue hang out, and panted like a dog, ---pretending to be tired.

The new route crossed a heavily traveled highway. The squirrel shot quickly across the road, lucky this time. On the other hand, while T.C. was being playful in his persuit, he made a mistake that for him was unheard of. Imagine! He misjudged the distance!

Before he had time to clear the last lane, a giant rig came roaring past. And T.C. the clever, T.C. the careful, T.C. who had never used up any of his nine lives, ran right into the hard black rubber of a rear truck tire.

The trucker had seen it happen in his side mirror. He quickly hit his brakes and switched on lots of blinking red and yellow lights to warn other drivers, and pulled into the emergency parking lane, stopping as soon as he could. Jumping out of the cab, he ran back to the point of impact.

There, on a yellow line, in the middle of the

He misjudged the distance!

highway, lay the limp body of a knocked out adventurer! The kind truck driver picked up the cat. It was still breathing! It didn't appear to have any broken bones, and there was no sign of blood.

"We'll get you fixed up," the man told T.C. "I'll drop you off at the animal clinic in Santa Barbara. Meanwhile, you just rest right here." He gently placed T.C. beside him on the cab seat.

It's a good thing the cat couldn't hear what the man was saying to him. He would have had a cat fit! Santa Barbara is north, not south. Like it or not, T.C.

Tom Cat was unconscious. Yet, -----

was headed farther away from his beloved Redondo Beach Pier, every second.

Tom Cat was unconscious. Yet, some part of his brain was still active, and it seemed to him he was in a very strange realm, having a very strange experience.

The cat found himself walking down a straight pathway strewn with pale yellow flower petals. Lights of every color of the rainbow, danced about him. He felt wonderful!

Soon he met a small white dog with friendly baby blue eyes, wearing a magnificent diamond collar.

"They are waiting for you sir," the dog said merrily to the cat.

"What? Who is waiting for me? No one here knows me. What is this place?" the cat demanded.

"You are headed in the right direction," the dog

smiled. "Just stay on the path!"

"The right direction to where?" T.C. was puzzled.

The little dog gave T.C. a pleasant glance, over his shoulder, as he trotted on.

What a peculiar situation, Tom Cat thought. He was lost in amazement! This calm, peaceful, totally lovely place, took his breath away! Since he had nothing better to do, he took the dog's advice and continued down the path.

Suddenly the path led to a neatly trimmed acreage. There were two red barns that looked very familiar, but out of place. The barns were identical in size and color. The strangest thing about this property was that there was no house! To the sides and rear of the barns, T.C. could see fresh green pastures and apple orchards. Delicious looking apples, of every description, hung from the branches. Also, there was a stream, a winding stream, flowing lazily in its mossy banks. A tidy fence looked familiar, and so did the gate! That green gate! Where had he seen it?

Then, without warning, the dream took a surprising turn. A barn door opened and there they were! It was them! Tom Cat stood in awe! How graceful! More beautiful than ever! Two familiar figures came toward him.

"Priscilla! Hotsie!" he whispered faintly. "You are supposed to be de---"

"T.C., I've missed you! How good to see you

again," Priscilla said happily. "Don't be afraid to say it. If you believe us to be dead, then we must be dead! Not as bad as you had supposed, right? To get here is like walking through a new door. All of a sudden, there you are!" Now, Priscilla looked squarely at the speechless cat. "You are a very special cat, T.C. Because of your kindness to others, you've been allowed to visit us. Not many just visit! As soon as you have been given your mission, you must return immediately!"

"You *must* get back to the farm, Tom Cat," Hotsie told him, with a sense of urgency in her voice. "There are so many problems! Things are going to get worse! Return at once! They need you there!"

"Look who's talking!" T.C. felt a little braver now. "You left! Priscilla left! Why don't you girls go back? And by the way, *if you are dead, what am I?*" The cat's eyes snapped from side to side.

Hotsie and Priscilla looked at each other and laughed. They don't look dead to me, Tom Cat thought. He was more than pleased to see that they were together and happy.

"How do you know about problems back on the farm?" T.C. asked. "You two haven't been hanging around there, have you?" The thought made him uneasy.

"We are not as far away as you might think!" Priscilla answered. "Don't worry. No one ever sees us!"

"It's almost time," Hotsie said.

"Time for what?" the cat asked.

"Listen, my friend. Listen carefully!" Priscilla became quite serious. *"In a few minutes you will awaken with a terrible headache, but it won't last long. Head north, to the farm. Little Prissy needs you, just as I did. But you must hurry! Get there before the storm!"*

T.C. *did* listen. Why me, he thought? What storm? And how do they know so much? But suddenly, the questions weren't important. There was something else to deal with.

Tom Cat had a terrible headache. He felt as though he'd been hit by a truck. Would he be able to get back to the farm in time?

Chapter 9.

HEADING BACK

Slowly, Tom Cat opened his eyes. For all he knew there could be more surprises awaiting him. His head really throbbed! Nothing else hurt! There were no legs missing. His tail was still attached! Ears, whiskers? He took inventory of all his bodily parts.

"Hey! What's going on here? I don't remember asking you for a ride." He glanced up at the truck driver who was busy watching the road.

"I've got to get out of here," T.C. told himself. "What if we're going south? This gear jammer is driving pretty fast!"

He could not explain his visit with Priscilla and Hotsie, *but he knew that they knew something he didn't.* He trusted them. No, this was not the time for going south to his beloved "fish heaven".

Although he didn't know it, the cat *was*

headed north. All he had to do was stay put! But the window was open. In one powerful thrust he bolted up and out through the opening! The driver was shocked to see this crazy, daring cat running in the opposite direction. It was apparent his passenger had made a miraculous recovery.

"No use to worry about him," the driver said out loud.

Perhaps it was the pain in his head that marred Tom Cat's sense of direction. He was not fooled for very long. After running a short distance in the wrong direction, he noticed his shadow was not where it should be. It was on the wrong side! Scrud! He was running south! That's pretty dumb, he thought. He stopped for a minute, hoping to clear up the faulty function of his brain. It's not easy to think when you have been hit by a truck, he was finding out!

T.C.'s accident happened in Malibu Beach. His truck ride carried him north to a spot near Ventura on Highway 101. Now he was surrounded by cotton fields. To his left were men and equipment. Near by, a field cat toyed with a mouse. Tom Cat needed information. The best source was from one of his kind. Obligingly, the field cat recommended that T.C. hitch a ride with Alfredo, whose pickup truck was parked nearby. Alfredo would be leaving in a few minutes. He'd go through Simi Valley and on over to Saugus to deliver vegetables. Saugus was on I-5, the main highway north.

"Good luck," wished the field cat. "You'll not have any problems catching a ride in Saugus. Lots of cars and trucks stop there."

Tom Cat hurried across the field to where Alfredo's pickup truck stood, loaded and ready to go. Up sprang the cat! He searched for a spot to ride where he would be hidden from human eyes. He found an empty crate with blue packing material in the bottom. Perfect! T.C. curled up in the crate and slept all the way to Saugus. When he woke up, the headache was almost gone.

Two young men were unloading the truck. They were laughing and speaking half the time in Spanish and the other in English. One of them sang a song about a cockroach. T.C. hoped the fellow hadn't seen one on the pick-up! He hated the nasty little insects!

Once on the ground, T.C. could see the entrance to I-5 north. Then something even more interesting caught his eye. Oregon license plates, ---on a bright red pickup and camper. It was parked off to the side of the entrance, heading the way he wanted to go. At present, the little vehicle suffered from a very flat tire! A man and a woman hustled around in the gravel, installing the tire.

T.C. kept out of their sight, but managed to spring gracefully from the gravel to the hood of the truck, then on to the roof of the camper. There were

T.C. spotted Oregon license plates.

several places to ride. He chose a woolen blanket tucked between suitcases tied firmly to a metal roof rack. He was hidden and within a few minutes, asleep again.

A few hours later, Tom Cat woke up suddenly when he realized they were no longer moving. They were stopped at a roadside rest to get some sleep. The man and woman stepped inside the camper. When he was sure they were asleep, T.C. went shopping for hand-outs. The rest area was well lighted. There were diners at several of the picnic tables. A couple of dogs were walking their owners.

In less than an hour, T.C. had eaten fried chicken with two friendly families, had half a ham and cheese sandwich shared by a young boy who was scheming to get rid of it, refused orange soda, and enjoyed a full cup of milk with bits of bacon in it. Where did he put it all? Food usually made him sleepy. Not this time.

What a day! So much had happened, most of which he could not explain. I'm going home, he thought. For the past weeks he had occasionally allowed himself to think about going home, only each time to remember the tragic death of his friend. He just had not been ready. Now things were different. He had seen her, somehow. She had said he must go home.

By sun up Tom Cat had returned to his bed on top of the camper. How lucky to get this ride. It sure beat walking!

About noon the driver pulled into the parking lot to a restaurant near Sacramento. Cat's nose told him so, he didn't even have to look. Familiar aromas thrilled his nostrils. Roast beef! Shrimp! Clams! Haddock! T.C. licked his lips!

It wasn't easy to wait until the driver and his wife were inside the cafe. But he did. T.C. was hungry.

Quickly, he jumped down and hurried around to the back door of the building. The kitchen door was open. Tom Cat was too smart to go inside. He waited.

An overweight lady scraped leftovers from plates into a tall gray can lined with plastic. Her cheeks were painted with a bright orange.

T.C. made a pitiful faint sound. Being demanding with loud meowings doesn't get you half as much as sounding like you're about to starve to death and looking like you'd be satisfied with any old crumb. Again he cried his mournful cry, turning sad eyes toward the lady.

Her heart melted. "Nice kitty, hungry kitty. Just stay there and I'll fix you a nice paper plate full of fish!"

How clever he was. Soon again his belly was full. He meandered back to the camper to wait. There was plenty of time. Eating with knives and forks takes longer. Must be a real nuisance, T.C. thought. There was shade under the little truck. He picked a spot to stretch out and let his lunch settle. Suddenly, he felt lonely, and wished with all his heart that his journey was over.

After a cat nap, he made his way back up to his perch. Just before his head hit the blanket, he heard a scratching noise. It sounded as though it came from the small window of the camper. T.C. hung his head over the side to have a look. And when he did he

"What are you doing up there?"

nearly fell off the truck. For what he saw sent him into a tizzy! Two lovely eyes stared up at him from the window. Female, ---cat eyes!

"What are you doing up there?" the gorgeous creature asked shyly.

T.C. could not take his eyes off her! "Why don't you come on up and find out?" he flirted.

"The Killians wouldn't like it," she said.

"Well I'm hitching a ride to Oregon," he told her. "You are headed for Oregon aren't you?" he grinned.

"Yes. That is, we're going on through Oregon to Washington for a while. Then we'll go back to our home in Oregon," she answered kindly.

T.C. imagined how nice it would be to ride inside

with this beautiful cat. To accomplish it, he would have to work fast. The driver and his wife would be back soon. He tried the direct approach.

"I've been traveling since spring. Now I must get back to the farm in Oregon, soon. It's very important! Could I ride inside with you?"

"No, you'd better not. My owners would be furious. They don't like to have any other cats around me," she told him. "Especially, males!"

He tried his second approach. "You are the loveliest creature I have ever seen." T.C. had said these words before, to other good looking cats, but this time he really meant it. "Please let me ride inside with you," he smiled pleasantly.

She hesitated. "I don't think so," she said.

T.C. was getting desperate. "But it's bumpy, --- and lonesome up there," he said with pleading eyes.

"Well, all right. But you'll have to hurry. I'm taking an awful chance! Can you possibly squeeze through the tear in the screen?" she asked.

Could he? What do you think? If it wasn't big enough he would make it a little bigger. Quickly, and with great expertise, he slithered through the tear. He was inside! Wow! What luck!

Right away Tom Cat scouted the interior for a hiding place. No problem. There were dozens.

Well, now, this is more like it, T.C. thought. He could not believe his good fortune. Standing next to this grand female, he began to examine her more closely. Fur as white as he imagined angel wings to be. Her eyes were pale blue, like the tiny feather he had once seen fall from a blue bird's nest. And she was as shy as the first day of school.

"By the way," he smiled a charming smile, "they call me T.C. That's short for Tom Cat."

"My name is Leeza," she purred.

When she said her name, Tom Cat was sure the door to his heart flew open.

Speaking of doors, someone was opening the back door to the camper, T.C. darted behind a bench.

"Here, kitty," said Mrs. Killian. She poured milk in one side of a two compartment dish. The other side was about half full of dry cat food. "Are you enjoying the trip, Leeza?" she asked. But before the cat could answer, the lady shut the door and soon, they were rolling down the road again.

"Boy! That was close!" T.C. exclaimed. "The last thing I want to do is get you into trouble!"

"We'll have to be very careful. If they see you, they'll kick you out!" Leeza seemed sad. "I get awfully lonesome. It will be nice to have someone to talk to."

"Why don't you ride up front with them?" T.C. asked. "If you belonged to me, I'd want you with me all the time." It was no secret how he felt about her.

"You don't understand sir," Leeza explained,

"I'm not a pet to the Killians. People are anxious to pay a lot of money for Angora cats like me. They breed me to prize winning males and sell my kittens. They call the money 'petty cat cash'."

"Why do you stay? Why don't you escape?" T.C. was serious.

"I wouldn't know what to do. Believe me, I've given it some thought! At least they feed me. I don't get hungry," she said, looking at her feeding dish. "You must be starved, T.C. I have enough for both of us."

Tom Cat looked first at the dry cat food and then at the milk. Poor girl, he thought. The next time we stop for food, I'll teach her how to eat! The miles passed swiftly, as he talked to Leeza about his travels and the farm. He shared his experience of seeing Priscilla and Hotsie.

By late afternoon, they were in northern California. While the Killians relaxed over an early supper, Leeza learned about back doors to kitchens and kind people. After supper the Killians drove to Medford, Oregon, where they spent the night. This time T.C. had company when he went exploring the rest area. There were the usual handouts, and trees to climb.

"My owners would have a fit if they knew I was out," Leeza whispered. T.C. could see she was worried, so he took her back to the camper to sleep.

Morning came and the little rig was again moving

north. T.C. knew that if all went well, he should arrive at the farm, by evening. Leaving Leeza would not be easy. He liked her a lot. He told her how he planned to get to the farm. He'd get off the camper, still on I-5, and take a certain county road home. Leeza listened carefully, as though she was making a mental note.

"I'll steal her," Tom Cat thought. "I'll take her to the farm with me." But he knew he shouldn't. "After all, she's safe here," he told himself, "and she's delicate, not a barn cat like me."

This was unusual thinking for T.C. He was a handsome cat and he knew it, but now, he was so impressed with this beautiful Angora, that he felt quite plain. Imagine. And after all, she had told him her home was in Albany, not far from the farm. He promised he would come and see her.

It didn't look as if Mr. Killian planned on stopping anywhere near T.C.'s turn-off. He would have to jump. No problem. He'd done it before.

Leeza watched as Tom Cat flung himself through the window. He landed on all fours, got up and waved good-bye with his plumey tail.

He was going home. What would he find? Would he ever see Leeza again?

T.C. waved good-bye.

Chapter 10.

T.C. RETURNS

By the time Tom Cat reached the farm, the evening sun had dropped behind the mountains. Chores had been over with for several hours; peace and quiet reigned. A few clouds had begun to form. The sows welcomed the cooler evening and were napping. Except for the grunt of a newborn pig here and there, all was silent.

T.C. trotted through the big front door of the farrowing barn, just as if he had never been away. No one heard his soft footfall or noticed as he climbed skillfully to the wood frames above the pens and worked his way up to his favorite old perch in the rafters. He was directly above what used to be Priscilla's pen.

He was a tuckered out cat. It had been a long time since he slept in his favorite spot. He slept a peaceful sleep, and dreamed wonderful dreams of a beautiful Angora cat with gentle blue eyes.

Little Prissy was asleep on her straw. T.C. didn't mind not being noticed. In fact, he had planned it that way. All he wanted for now, was sleep!

Tom Cat had no immediate plans except to look the situation over. Then, he'd try to figure out why he was needed. And, what about this storm Hotsie and Priscilla had mentioned? It wasn't even raining! Had it all been a dream, perhaps a nightmare? If T.C. believed that, he would never have come home, at least not yet, but would have headed straight for Redondo Beach and fish heaven!

Morning burst forth with color and sound, as though someone just turned up the volume on the stereo. There were anxious appeals. Waiting for breakfast, which hadn't arrived yet, always brought on anxious appeals in the hog barn.

The morning sun poked beams of light through the windows and doors. Touched by the rays the wheat straw became elegant. The sows lay on beds of shimmering gold. Now and then a cloud made its way in front of the sun and robbed the shadows.

Breakfast arrived on time. Papa and Mama hurried from pen to pen with feed and water. Sounds of eating filled the air. When the chores were done, Mama stopped by Little Prissy's pen to say hello.

"You are looking good this morning, Prissy!" Mama said cheerfully as she entered the pen.

Prissy grunted a greeting,
And, kept on with her eating.

Mama tried again, "You're due to have your pigs in about three weeks, Prissy." Prissy continued eating.

"You don't really care, do you?" Mama laughed. "Papa cares. Papa says that you are going to be his next pig producing champion, like Hotsie was. You do remember Hotsie, don't you?" Mama teased, trying to get Prissy to stop eating and talk to her.

"I remember her," Prissy said, with a mouth full of food. "She was my mother's best friend. I was just a baby then, but I remember the night she died. My mother cried a lot about it."

"I know she did, darling. So did I. Papa too."

Perhaps you think it's strange that Mama and Little Prissy understand each other, but it all seemed quite natural to them. Before they could continue with their conversation, they heard Papa shout.

"T.C.!" Papa cried from outside the barn door, "Is that you?" Tom Cat jumped up in Papa's arms, and rubbed his head against Papa's chin. It was hard to tell which was the happier.

Mama heard Papa's cry, Little Prissy heard it and so did all the sows who were close up front. But news travels quickly in the farrowing barn, soon everyone would know. Mama scrambled over the pen and out to see for herself if it was really true. Sure enough!

There he was!

"Oh, Tom Cat, you've come home at last! Where did you go? How did you live? Who took care of you?" Mama kept asking questions and thought of a lot more. But the cat just made happy purring sounds as Papa stroked his back. There was a tear in Papa's eye.

To answer Mama's questions would be useless. Mama would not understand him anyway. Eventually, she would find out. T.C. would tell Prissy, and Prissy always told Mama almost everything.

Tom Cat was home. He was the king of cats, on this farm. And as king, he could do anything he wished. Right now, he had "strutting in" on his mind. After all, he was a V.I.P. Hadn't he and Priscilla been the best of friends? Hadn't he been her mouth piece, going here and there, sharing her stories of television shows, trips to southern California and Las Vegas? And he had done it so well, he told himself, ---with expert deliverance in each and every performance.

He would be cool, casual and confident as he made his grand entrance back into the farrowing barn. Papa had set the stage by announcing his return.

T.C. could just imagine what the sows were saying about him. How they had missed him. About his great talents and courage. But above all, he supposed they would be discussing his "handsomeness". He was ready for their cheers and shouts. Should he strut?

Should he be nonchalant?

After all his careful planning, ---he blew it all. He spoiled his chance to show off. But he could wait no longer. For he truly loved Little Prissy and was dying to tell her how much he had missed her.

Down he jumped, from Papa's arms. After a few broad leaps forward, he slithered gingerly through the boards of Little Prissy's pen.

"Well, look who's back!" Prissy commented casually.

T.C. was quite taken aback and somewhat disappointed that he was not being greeted with more enthusiasm by his favorite "Little Porker".

"I thought you'd be glad to see me!" he announced.

"I'm glad you're back, Tom Cat. I really am. But if I get too glad about it, you might just up and leave again," Little Prissy said shyly. "Nearly everybody I call friend or family either hits the road, or dies! Hotsie died, all my brothers and sisters died, my mother died, you left and then Mitzi died!"

"What? Mitzi is dead?" T.C. sounded sad and surprised.

"Oh, I'm sorry T.C. I forgot she died after you left."

"How did she die? When did it happen?" he asked.

"Mitzi was with Priscilla when she died. The little

dog refused to eat after that." Prissy told him. "When Mama and Papa left the barn that night, they noticed Mitzi was not with them. She had not jumped into the car like she always did. Papa came back inside to look for her. She was always in Priscilla's pen. That's where he found her, there in my mother's pen." Prissy nodded toward the front pen. "She was shaking and whining. Papa went into the pen to see what was wrong. That's when he discovered that my mother was, ---" Prissy tried hard to hold back the tears, but she could not. "She was dead, T.C."

"I know, Prissy. I was here, and I was in her pen. Priscilla knew she was dying, but she held on until all your pigs were born. Even when she was dying, she still didn't want to be troublesome. You know how she was. She told me and Mitzi good-bye. Afterwards, I went up to my perch in the rafters and spent the night. Just before daylight, I took off. I should have stayed around long enough to tell you how sorry I felt for you, Prissy. I guess I was feeling too sorry for myself. I should have stayed with you, but I took the easy way out and ran away." The cat was feeling a-shamed of himself.

"Mitzi died about six weeks later. She had grieved herself to death. Mama and Papa buried her back in the timber, beside Priscilla. But let's not talk about that anymore." Prissy said anxiously.

T.C. had decided not to tell Little Prissy about

having seen Priscilla and Hotsie, nor about their instructions to him. After all, who would believe him? He intended to snoop around, ask questions and find out what was going on around there that required his stately presence. Suddenly, he realized there was no sound in the barn. There was an uncanny quiet. The sows were listening, trying to catch every word of what he had supposed was a private conversation.

He spun around! Up to the top boards of Prissy's pen he flew to get a better look. Now, the greeting that he had sought became a reality.

What a warm, wonderful welcome it was. Mabel and Rachel on either side of Prissy's pen were the only ones who could actually hear T.C. and Prissy's conversation. It was all right that they heard. After all, they were very good old friends. They greeted him. So did Blossom, Charlie the boar, young Carlotta, Peaches, Rachel and others. Even the young sows, new in the barn, had heard about this entertaining tabby and took delight in his return.

T.C. slipped in and out of a few pens spending a minute or two in cheery greetings. He worked his way back to Charlie's pen. Charlie was a good natured fellow, a friend to all. Usually, he had a first hand account of everything of importance that took place in the farrowing barn.

Before putting it out of his mind completely, T.C. allowed himself one negative thought. What if the trouble is too much for one cat to handle? What then?

Chapter 11.

INFORMATION

I'm glad you're back, safe and looking as great as ever," Charlie smiled.

"I thank you sir," T.C. bowed a low, cross legged bow. "Now that I'm home, I'm rather glad about it myself! You should have been with me, Charlie."

"Oh yeah? I don't think so! I've heard about cats. You can go anywhere! But us hogs, ---well, we'd get eaten for breakfast. No, thank you! I'll stay right where I am. It may be dull sometimes, but it's better than ending up as bacon on some fat lady's table."

"I see your point, Charlie," T.C. grinned.

"Prissy could use some cheering up, Tom Cat." Charlie became serious. He spoke in low tones. "The sows shun her because she's so much smarter than they are. She's so much like her mother. She wants to be liked. I don't know why that matters. It doesn't

71

seem to matter to anybody else. You remember that temper she used to have? It's gone. It's like her fire went out when she heard that nasty rumor."

"What rumor?" This was the first time T.C. had heard about it.

"I'll let her tell you my friend. But I will tell you one thing, this rumor is bad. It's destroying Little Prissy. She thinks of little else. Before the rumor, when anyone dared to cross her, she didn't care. In fact, she'd tell 'em off. She'd say something that I'm sure you taught her when she was little. 'Ask me if I care'."

Tom Cat grinned and nodded.

"But now, ---well, it's like she's given up on everything and everybody. Maybe you can help her, if you can win her trust again." Charlie lowered his voice more, even to a whisper. He truly hoped that T.C. would know what to do.

"You are here to stay, aren't you?" he asked.

"Yes. I'm here to stay," was the cat's simple answer. "See ya, Charlie." With that farewell, the cat climbed, leaped, and climbed some more, until he reached the uppermost rafters in the barn. He wanted a place to think.

"What is going on here?" T.C. pondered. He could rush right down and ask Little Prissy. Maybe she wasn't ready to tell him and he didn't want to be pushy. Not with Little Prissy. He could rush right

down and ask anybody. If it was a rumor, then everybody knew it, except "himself". Then the cat said to
himself, "Self, the time has come to use your smarts!"
He vowed he would know what the rumor was, by
noon. And, he vowed he would get the information
without having to ask for it. That was his decision.

The cat realized he had made a big mistake by
climbing up. Heat rises. He was just about as high as a
cat could ever get. It was scorching hot up there.
Quickly, and oh so gracefully, down and out, he flew.
Out to the pasture where there were shade trees and a
cool stream. Also, out there, somewhere, he'd find
Victoria. Victoria was a wise old sow, good natured
and kind, even if she was a trifle cantankerous sometimes.

Tom Cat had an idea where she'd be. There was a
bit of paradise in the pasture, just perfect for days
such as this. A narrow stream trickled under the gran-
daddy of all pine trees. Low-hanging branches pressed
the earth. Only a sliver of sun crept in under the tree.

Victoria rested on a moist, mossy knoll in this
wonderful shady spot. She was delighted to have the
company of this cat who had once again cast anchor
in her domain. Before breakfast she had spoken to
him briefly. He had been preoccupied while stalking a
fat field mouse. Victoria had watched and grazed.

Now they talked and renewed their friendship. At first Victoria spoke of old times. T.C. graciously allowed her that pleasure. But very soon T.C. sashayed the topic of conversation around to the present. And to be more specific, Little Prissy's present. How clever he was. For the very thing he wanted to know, was the next thing that came out of the old sow's mouth.

"They're going to sell her, you know. As long as she's here, she's a constant reminder to them of Priscilla."

"Sell her? Sell Little Prissy? Impossible! They would never do a thing like that! Does Mrs. 'C' still spend time in Prissy's pen, like she always did?" he asked.

"Yes, quite often in fact," Victoria answered.

"You see? Someone is playing a bad joke on Prissy and I'm going to find out who it is." T.C. was furious. Victoria had never seen such an outburst of emotion from this fellow. The cat mumbled curses and promised vengeance against this unknown enemy.

"No wonder the Little Porker is tormented." T.C. shouted. The wind responded to his anger! Gusts of hot air swirled around them and bolted up through the tree. Victoria became frightened. The low-hanging branches swayed boldly, sweeping the ground. And then it was still again.

"That was a warning," Victoria announced,

gazing upward. "A warning always comes ahead of great danger. I've lived a lot of years, T.C. I can tell you, we're in for some kind of trouble. Bad trouble."

The planning going on in Tom Cat's head left little room to take heed to Victoria's warning. Normally, on such a day, the cat would have stayed in the shade and slept. But today would not be a normal day. In fact, today would be a day that none of them would ever forget. Heat or no heat, T.C. had something he had to do.

How did Priscilla and Hotsie know? He kept asking himself the same question, over and over.

Now there was another question of equal importance. Who hated Prissy enough to start this horrible rumor? A spine-chilling possibility flashed into his head! Maybe there was yet more to know. After all, he had been gone for a long time. Maybe it was not a rumor!

Chapter 12.

THE STORM HITS

he water sprinklers on the roof were turned up full blast. Papa had them installed for hot days such as this. Cooling the barn, even by just a few degrees, was helpful. The thermometer now read 96, and climbing.

Although the sows were uncomfortable, they could stand a lot of heat.

Once again Little Prissy had overturned her drinking water, on purpose. Others had done the same. They would rather have a wet spot to lie on than a lot

of water for drinking. With Prissy three weeks away from her delivery date, she was a mass of hog. The moist wood floor offered a few minutes of cooling luxury to her belly.

Prissy was a thoughtful hog. In spite of her own discomfort at times, she was more concerned about Mabel. Mabel wasn't young anymore. Her pigs were due in three days. She was larger and more effected by the heat than Prissy.

"I sure hope this hot weather goes away before Sunday, Mabel," Prissy said kindly, as she peeked between the 2x4's that divided their pens. "Your new babies might not like the heat."

"Don't worry about me, child! I've had pigs in the hot weather before. Besides, I've got it all planned. I intend to have my litter on Saturday night when things have cooled off a bit." She said good humoredly. "But you know how it is, Prissy. When the sweet little things are ready to be born, ---that's when they're born." Her's was the voice of experience.

"Isn't that the truth! Now, about me. I figure I've got a few weeks left around here before they sell me," Prissy said sadly. "Since I'm still here and my pigs are due in three weeks, I live in hope that they will keep me until after the weaning, ---that's another five weeks. So, I figure the best I can hope for is about eight more weeks. But who knows, Mabel, at at any moment a truck could back up to that loading chute. I'd be gone. Gone forever, my friend." A lone tear trickled down her face. "I'll miss you Mabel, and I'll miss Charlie. I'll miss this pen, ---my home."

"Don't think about it Prissy. Maybe it won't happen." The wise old sow changed the subject.

"Isn't it nice having Tom Cat home?"

"I guess so," Prissy blubbered.

Tom Cat was in, ---and out. He was "in" listening to private conversations, expecting to hear Prissy's name mentioned. He was "out" scouting for answers to his question in other places. He was an experienced snooper. He would succeed. He had told himself so. Fail? Never! Failure, for this proud cat, would not be possible.

Prissy watched with great curiosity as the cat meandered about.

"What do you suppose he's up to, Mabel?" Prissy asked.

"Who knows? He'll be by, directly. Likely as not he'll fill you in on what he's been doing."

All afternoon Prissy poured over the cat's activities. A half dozen times she woke Mabel just to tell her how peculiar she thought the cat was acting. The hot afternoon passed rather quickly. Wondering what the cat was up to left no time for her to think about her own problems.

By four o'clock the sky was all puffed up with grayish, billowy clouds. The clouds became restless.

They began to move with the breeze, to roll and to gather. For a time the sky turned yellowish and dirty looking. Afterwards, the wind picked up. Dust began to whiff along the ground forming odd shaped dust devils here and there.

Mama and Papa arrived to do the chores about the time the wind really began to blow. The situation worsened. Lightning zigzagged across the sky, ripping as it went.

Quickly, Papa dragged a canvas tarp out front to cover a stack of baled bedding straw. Mama hurried to help as the tarp flapped and waved and flew up over Papa's head. Mama laughed as she competed with the wind for the tarp. A sudden gust of air ballooned the canvas, jerking it out of their hands. Across the gravel it rolled and popped, beating the earth. It picked up speed! Papa ran, with arms swinging wildly, to catch it. Finally, he caught up and planted both feet firmly on it's top side. Now, the two of them held on tightly until the tarp was securely tied around the straw.

"Jim Bosley said something about a heat storm, but I don't remember anything about this gale!" Papa was hollering. Jim Bosley was Papa's favorite T.V. weatherman. More often than not, this fellow was right about the weather.

Down the hallway Papa hurried to check on a couple of sows. Mama wasted no time in getting in

The storm blew in.

Prissy's pen. She carried in a feed bucket, turning it upside down to make a place to sit.

"It's been a long hot day, Prissy, but I guess you know that already," she smiled.

Prissy looked at Mama and was puzzled. "Doesn't the thunder and lightning scare you even a little bit?" she asked slowly.

"Not much. But the wind, ---well, that's something else again." She reached for a brush that hung from a nail on the wall and stroked the little sow's back. "Have you noticed how fast it's cooling off, Prissy?"

"Yes! Does that scare you?" Prissy thought there must be something that Mama was afraid of. Prissy would never admit it to a soul. but she was truly afraid of storms. The rain did not bother her. Rain was a fact of life in Oregon. Usually, it fell quietly. But, thunder, and these fiery streaks in the sky bothered her a lot. And now, to add to her misery, there was wind.

"Yes, Prissy, I'm afraid of the wind when it gets like this. I've seen what it can do," Mama replied, hoping she had not added more fear for the little sow to handle.

The storm grew more deafening. Each flash of lightning brought forth more deep throated rumbles of thunder. Most of the sows slept right through it, enjoying the cooler air.

The newly born pigs were experiencing their first storm. Most of them were already hiding under their straw bedding. Now and then a courageous little soul would stick his head out for a moment. But as soon as the storm sounded, back he went.

Splash, a piglet belonging to Peaches, was having the biggest problem. He was cute and clever, but he was always getting into lots of trouble.

Papa named him Splash for an obvious reason. The little fellow loved water. He would climb over the side of the water tub and drop in. Splash! That's how he came by his odd name.

Little Prissy and Splash had something in common. Storms frightened them. Prissy had never outgrown her fear. Splash might, someday, ---he might not! At present, he was as close to his mother as a pig could ever get. If she should roll over, he'd be squashed.

"Thank goodness, there will be no babies born to-night," Papa announced as he approached Prissy's pen. "Let's get out of here, Mama, before it starts rainin'. Me thinks it's gonna pour! Soon! This will be a good night for T.V. and popcorn."

"That is, if the wind doesn't knock the power out." Mama was remembering a couple of times the electricity was off for three days because of wind storms. "Everything is O.K. here then? Are we through for the day, I hope?" Mama asked.

"This is a good ol' barn," Papa said, glancing about. "It will stand a lot of wind. We had better get goin', Mama. Is that all right with you, Prissy?"

Prissy did not answer Papa. She knew he could understand only a few words of her language. Only she and Mama could communicate freely.

Prissy looked into Mama's face. "It would be nice if you could stay a little while longer," she said, eyes pleading for the right answer.

It's hard to tell why one person is afraid of storms and another is not. Little Prissy was definitely fearful. How she dreaded being left alone in her pen.

Mama had not budged. She knew that Prissy was panicstricken, but if Prissy would not express her fears, then Mama would not let on that she knew.

Mama looked overhead for help. There he sat, looking back at her and reading her mind. Or, so it seemed.

The cat curled up in her feed trough.

"You're not alone, darling," she smiled with relief. "You are in where it's dry. Papa and I have to get to the house, so we will be too!"

As soon as they were out of sight, T.C. made his descent. The sight of the cat gave great comfort to Prissy. It brought back old memories too. She remembered how he used to drop in when she was a baby. He had been a friend one could depend on. The cat curled up in the feed trough. The storm became more powerful. Suddenly, rain pelted the metal roof, adding to the blatant force of nature's attack. Shattered lines of fire cracked across the heavens, followed by long piercing booms!

Dusk fell early with it's blanket of blackness.

No one, absolutely no one, would expect a visitor on such a night. Right?

A tousled gray, wet streak shot nervously through the front door. Piston! He brayed loud bellows, head up-turned, as if he were pleading with the sky. The burro had announced his arrival.

"What is that?" T.C. shouted with enough volume to be heard by everybody, above the racket of the storm. Piston was a newcomer to T.C.

"That, is trouble! He's Greystone's adopted bur-ro. I think they'd like for him to adopt someone else! He's a real troublemaker, ---gets out all the time," Prissy told him. "His name is Piston." T.C. laughed!

"Papa says the name suits him," Prissy continued. "He said that a piston was something that moves around a lot. One thing about this burro, he really gets around!"

Tom Cat gawked at Piston and laughed again. Piston did not like being laughed at. The burro did look comical, with wet hair stuck tight to his skin. He resembled an overgrown mouse. T.C. was sure he had seen the shadow of a small mouse on the wall one night that looked just like this beast.

For a while at least, Prissy forgot to be afraid. Her mind was on the uninvited guest. What kind of trouble would he stir up, tonight?

Chapter 13.

A NIGHT OF TROUBLE

Piston jogged a short distance down the center hallway, looking around at nobody in particular. Tonight he was greeted with unusual hostility. To Charlie and the sows, the burro's being there meant trouble! He was not to be trusted, ever.

Piston wasn't really an evil fellow, and he didn't go out looking for trouble. The problem was, he just couldn't seem to avoid it.

Some of the sows who were already uneasy because of the hullabaloo of the storm's racket told themselves they could not welcome this annoying creature. Not here! Not tonight! And why did he have to pick this particular spot to visit?

Mabel was busy, as always, doing what she did best, ---being a kind, loving soul. She remembered Little Prissy's fear of storms and was determined to do something about it. The sound of the rain on the roof made the aging sow sleepy, but she fought it off. She kept up a cheery conversation with Prissy and T.C.

The friendly cat had curled up close to Little Prissy. He wondered. Is *this* the storm? Is this the one I was warned about by Priscilla and Hotsie? If it is, what's the problem? A storm is a storm. The barn was still standing, even though whips of wind caused the timbers to rub and to moan. What was the big deal? Was he here just to comfort Prissy? Perhaps. After all, her fear was great and very real.

Today's snooping had not been a total loss. Several times he had overheard mention of the rumor, a couple of times in the feeder building. Some young gilts were talking. Gilts are teen age hogs. Two of them, he discovered, were Prissy's daughters, Patsy and Penny. How lovely they were, and intelligent, and well bred, and, why shouldn't they be, ---after all, they were Little Prissy's daughters, and Priscilla's granddaughters. He felt sad, seeing them now for the first time. They were nearly grown, and he hadn't been around to see them grow up. Perhaps he could make up for it, he thought. He would get to know them, soon, and become their friend.

And, while he evesdropped in secret, up in the hot rafters above the sows, Prissy's name was mentioned several times. Surprisingly, there were no unkind words about his "Little Porker"! If she had an enemy, and he was sure she did, he would find the culprit.

For a few seconds the storm made no sound. No lightning flashed. No thunder roared. At most, a gentle rain fell noiselessly to the ground.

What a relief! Prissy hoped with all her heart that it was over, gone forever.

But in the twinkling of a truth, her hopes were shattered. The storm burst forth with deafening fury. Lightning crashed and cracked. It shot in all available directions and split the heavens. The thunder answered with low boilings over and around and under and behind. It spoke from every corner of the sky and then exploded into long lasting, piercing booms. The farrowing barn shook violently. Windows rattled.

"Why doesn't it stop?" Prissy cried.

There was someone else reacting to the boom. The burro, who was standing in front of Rosie's pen, began to spin like a top. Around and around he whirled. Suddenly, as if the whirling was not enough, he bucked and brayed mournful, tormented sounds. As he spun, he kicked straight out with both hind feet. Everything that came into contact with the amazingly powerful blows, went crashing to the ground. Both main supporting posts to Rosie's pen slammed down. Rosie cried out! Had she been hit? Was she hurt or just frightened?

Crash! ---went Prissy's gate and part of the wall to

The burro began to spin like a top.

her pen. Down the alley way, the burro whacked and banged like a bucking bronco at a rodeo. One collision after another.

Peaches had but one lower 2"x4" remaining on the front of her pen. Mabel's gate was broken loose, hanging on a single hinge. Both Carlotta and Rachel had been freed and now ran aimlessly around in the hallway. Pigs ran in every direction. No one was more confused than Piston, who now stood still. A trickle of blood ran down one hind leg and he limped on the other.

"Oh! Boy! Will Papa be mad!" Prissy shouted.

Shouts of anger fell on deaf ears of the burro. Even quiet, sober-minded Charlie was yelling threats.

"Now get out of here, you crazy donkey, ---before you hurt somebody. Look what you've done!"

Pigs were running in and out of the building. Splash had crawled over the remaining 2"x4" on his pen and was free to run. The noisy little fellow crept into Mabel's pen through the gate hanging by one hinge.

"Go back to your pen, Splash. Stay with your mother. And watch out for the feet of that crazy, bucking burro." Mabel advised.

Piston heard. "I'm not crazy. The storm's crazy." he said.

"You see, Porker, you're not the only one who's afraid of storms." T.C. told her. "When the burro gets upset, he kicks."

"But, he should have gone outside to do it, Prissy answered. "He doesn't have very good manners, or sense." She looked at Piston standing there now with his head down and couldn't help feeling a little sorry for him.

"I don't think he meant any harm. Like he said, 'The storm's crazy', so, it makes him crazy too!'" T.C. suggested.

"Pretty smart thinkin' for a cat," Piston spoke up. His big ears served as a sensitive antenna.

T.C. couldn't believe the burro's hearing ability. With the storm blasting away, he had heard their comments. Since this was the first burro he'd ever known, T.C. really wasn't much of an authority on their hearing or anything else.

No pigs were left in the pens that had been kicked in. A few of them had run out of the building. All of Papa's pigs were used to confinement, not freedom. Papa had learned a long time ago that pigs like to run, ---halfway to the next county if they get a chance. These guys were getting their first taste of running free.

Now, Peaches, Carlotta and Rachel were all out looking for their pigs. Rain pattered down like a Gatlin gun on a battle field. The hogs were headed for the timber located on the back of the eighty acres. Once out of the building and across the pasture they could be safe under the shelter of the trees.

The troublemaker was not through making trouble. Piston responded to a sudden blaze that luminated the universe. Bang! Boom! Thunderous convulsions followed.

Spooked again, he crashed through Mabel's

busted gate.

"Get out of the way, Mabel," Prissy shouted.

The old sow tried. She headed out, but her pace was slow and not in time. The burro's heels found their mark. He kicked her hard, in the side. Mabel fell to her knees and then to the floor in the hallway. She lay motionless.

"Mabel!" Prissy yelled."Get up, get up! He'll trample you!"

But the old sow couldn't get up. She struggled and tried her best. Prissy and T.C. hurried to her side. Prissy rooted at her back to lift her, while T.C. became a one man cheering section.

"Come on Mabel," he said. "You can do it! You have got to do it!"

Piston again stood still in the back corner of Mabel's pen and watched.

Mabel could not have gotten up without assistance. Finally, on her feet, she limped slowly into Prissy's pen and immediately laid down on the straw.

Prissy felt sure that Mabel was suffering, for when her body hit the straw, she groaned. Mabel never groaned.

Charlie, with his front feet resting on the top boards of his pen, watched. He had had enough.

"Donkey, you've had it!" he yelled as he vaulted his gate. Papa always said that Charlie could get out of that pen any time he wanted to. But he never did.

"Now go home, and don't come back!"

And now, he jumped out! Cedar shavings flew beneath his feet as he dug in. He raced wildly down the hallway, determination in every step.

A charging boar, as mad as Charlie, can do one of three things, ---kick, ---bite, or root. Charlie was not vicious, even now, and what he did looked pretty comical.

Charlie chased the frightened burro out into the hallway. Next, he rammed his head between Piston's hind legs, from behind. Then he raised up. When he did, the fainthearted beast looked like a wheelbarrow, with two front feet on the ground and the two hind legs dangling helplessly around Charlie's neck.

Charlie "wheeled" Piston out the front door, ran him out about twenty feet, gave him a wild toss with his strong head and yelled, "Now go home, and don't come back!" Charlie had done his duty.

Prissy watched. "I'll bet he comes back," she said.

Mabel suffered quietly on Prissy's straw. She was talking to Charlie, mumbling something, but he was just now coming back into the barn and was not aware of it.

Tom Cat called to Charlie who was receiving compliments for ridding the barn of the winner of the night's troublemaker award.

"Mabel is trying to tell you something, Charlie."

He stopped short in front of Prissy's pen. "Are you in pain, Mabel?" Charlie asked.

"He didn't mean to do it, Charlie. He was just scared of the storm. Some of us shake when we're scared, like the baby pigs. Some of us holler out loud. Piston, ---well, Piston kicks out. He did hurt me, Charlie, ---but by morning I'll be just fine, you'll see."

"Mabel, you never complain; even when you should, you don't. Are you sure you're all right? Would you tell us if you weren't?" Prissy asked.

"Don't worry about me, child," she answered. "I'm old and I'm tired. That's my biggest problem.

Let's hope that Rachel and Carlotta and Peaches are with their pigs, and that they are safe out there, where ever they are."

What a thoughtful, unselfish old sow she was. In all her suffering, she was more concerned about the problems of others. She had said that being old and tired were her biggest problems. This time she was wrong. The blow to her side was damaging, and she was in great pain.

All the havoc and harm to the building and hogs had happened in a matter of a few minutes. Papa and Mama had no way of knowing. They were probably in the house watching television and eating popcorn.

Charlie decided to lie down in the hall where he could keep and eye on the front door, just in case. Where he lay, he could also talk to Mabel.

Prissy hoped Mabel would be all right by Sunday, when her pigs were due to arrive. She thought about the other babies, out there in the storm, and wondered if they had gone to the shelter of the timber.

Chapter 14.

GETTING HELP

Prissy and T.C. rummaged around, checking on all the damage. The three front pens on Prissy's side of the building were defaced badly, ---in effect, wiped out, ---Mabel's, up front, Prissy's in the middle and Rachel's to her left. The same could be said for the three pens directly across the hall, ---Peaches's pen, up front, Carlotta's next and Rosie's third.

Rosie's gate and front fence were leaning in. The two main supporting posts were pointing towards the back. One was ripped loose from its foundation. Neither could be seen from the hallway.

"Rosie is sure quiet!" Prissy told T.C. "How can she sleep with all this racket going on?"

There was no opening to get in or out of her pen. Although the front was leaning, the gate and fence were all connected in one mass. Prissy peeked in. At first she didn't see Rosie, only beams and boards. Then something else caught her attention. Some of the straw was bright red. Red. Red?

"T.C., you'd better go in and see about her. I'm too big, but you can slip through easily." Prissy never took her eyes off the sow.

"Rosie, what's wrong?" Prissy asked sweetly.

Rosie did not answer.

Tom Cat carefully made his way in through the wreckage. From the looks of it, everything that could fall, had fallen on Rosie.

"Talk to us, Rosie! Where do you hurt? What can we do?" Prissy insisted. Her concern was genuine, for Prissy was a kind, caring hog. "See if you can get her to talk, Tom Cat. She won't ever talk to me. She doesn't like me."

"Well, she better talk now if she can. She's in bad shape. One front leg is bent backwards. It can't be that bent without being broken! And there's a humongous gash in her neck. She's a bloody mess, ---it's oozing out!"

That explained the red straw. It was Rosie's blood!

"It's too late," Rosie cried faintly, "nobody can help me. I'm going to die. Nobody could hear me when I was suffering. I cried out but nobody came to my rescue. But now, I don't hurt anymore. I don't feel anything. I suppose I'm nearly dead." She was sad indeed and had given up.

"Don't say that, Rosie, don't ever give up! Can you move at all?" Prissy asked.

"She can't move, Porker," T.C. answered, "there is too much weight on her and she's weak and all busted up. There's not much we can do for her; help won't be here until morning!"

"We've got to do something! We can't just let her lay there and bleed to death! And, I'm not waiting until morning, ---I don't care if she doesn't like me, that's her problem. I've got to get help for Mabel and Rosie too. I'm going to the house, now! Mama and Papa would want to be here. They know what to do. Somebody's got to tell them and I'm the only one who can." For a sow who was never listened to, Little Prissy's speech had definitely attracted attention!

"What! You can't go down there!" Charlie told her.

"Oh! Yes I can! I'm going and I'll come back with help."

"You will get lost out there in the dark, Prissy," Charlie told her. "You never go out in the dark," he insisted.

"She won't get lost," T.C. announced, "because I'm going with her. Dark never stopped me from going out at night. How do you suppose the expression 'Tom Catting' had it's beginning?" He grinned, "It was nice to have an activity named after me."

Charlie felt better knowing that this crazy, pompous cat was going along.

Mabel lay still, but not asleep. She was about as worried as a sow ever gets. In silence, she bore her pain. Now, even more anguish had come upon her, --- to place her in additional danger. Her labor had begun and no one must know. With so much misery all around, Mabel had decided to keep her problem to herself.

Little Prissy and Tom Cat wasted no time. They hurried across the orchard, splashing rainwater with every step. Prissy knew the way. She had walked it with Mama, many times. However, on this dark and dreary night it was good to have T.C.'s company.

The thunder and lightning had lessened. Still, enough was lurking around to make Prissy feel uneasy. It was pouring rain! That didn't bother her too much, but T.C. hated getting wet. After a few seconds, he looked as though he'd been dunked in the lake.

As the two of them neared the house, a dog began to bark. Prissy recognized the sound.

"Don't worry, it's just Maggie. Maggie always sounds her alarm when anyone gets near the house, even Papa and Mama," Prissy explained. This time Maggie wouldn't stop barking. A sow and a cat together, walking toward the house in the pouring rain, was not a usual sight.

Prissy and T.C. hurried to the farmhouse for help.

Little Prissy thought perhaps Papa would come out to investigate. She thought wrong. Papa was asleep in his rocker. Mama was working on her genealogy at the dining room table. Pedigree charts and family group sheets were stacked everywhere. All this would go into her Book of Remembrance.

Prissy could not open the door. If she had to, she could break it down, but she hoped that would not be necessary. Somehow, she must get their attention and do it quickly. She thought of Mabel and then of Rosie.

First she began to squeal, a long shrill cry. Maggie's bark merged into howls as she began running full circles around the sow. Not to be outdone, Tom Cat leaped for the living room window screen and hung on. He opened his mouth and let fly a series of spirited caterwauls, the kind usually reserved for fights. The kind that bring sensible people to their feet to do crazy things, ---like throwing Sunday shoes out the window in the rain, ---anything to stop that horrible racket!

Prissy continued to squeal. While she was good at it, apparently she was not good enough. She must try a new tactic. Around the house she raced and up onto the back porch.

"Mama," she squealed. "Mama, come quickly. Help!"

Papa's eyes flew open. Mama threw down her ball point pen and hurried to open the door.

"Prissy!" she exclaimed, surprised at what she saw on the back porch. "What did you say? And what are you doing here?"

Tom Cat tried to get their attention

Already, Papa was reaching for his slicker. "What did she say?" he asked Mama. If there was a hog on the back porch that should be in the barn then he knew there was work to do.

"Piston came and caused a lot of trouble! He kicked Mabel in the side and Rosie's pen has fallen in on her. We need you, ---bad!" Prissy told her. "There is more. Several sows and their pigs are out!"

Mama and Papa grabbed flashlights and rain gear and quickly sped out. As they made their way out to the farrowing barn, Prissy tried to fill Mama in on all the details of the evening; Mama in turn filled Papa in on all the details of the evening.

Papa got to the barn first. He turned on more lights.

"Oh! My! Would you look at this mess? Where's Mabel?" Her pen was empty!

"In Prissy's pen," Mama answered, "or what's left of it."

Mama climbed over Rosie's side wall, "We'll get you some help, girl. Oh! My! Papa, Rosie is hurt bad!"

"And Mabel is in labor. I'll call the vet!" Papa answered, heading for the phone in the storage room.

"Better call two young ones, looks like we'll be here all night!" Mama advised.

Very carefully, the two of them lifted the heavy timbers off Rosie's torn and broken body. The sow did not appear to notice. Was she dying? Was she past feeling? There was a pool of blood on the floor from the open gash in Rosie's neck. Most of the blood had dried. Maybe that's a good sign, Papa thought; perhaps the bleeding had stopped. "Her right front leg is busted up pretty bad," he said.

Not knowing what else to do, Charlie and Prissy and T.C. milled around in the hallway. With help on the scene, Charlie began to walk toward his pen. Papa saw him heading that way. He caught up to him and opened his gate.

"So you jumped over, huh? I owe you one, Charlie, for running off that infernal donkey! I'm gonna bring you a bucket full of the best apples in the orchard."

Charlie understood, and was glad his services had been noticed and appreciated.

Headlights of a car lit up the hallway. A neighbor, Will Harper, had seen the lights on in the barn and wondered if there had been wind damage.

"It's more like 'donkey damage', " Mama told him.

Mr. Harper rolled up his sleeves and went to work. Sheep was his business. Repairing buildings fell under that heading. He was an experienced, welcomed guest. No one had to tell him what to do. Papa pointed out the location of the tools and his neighbor went to work.

Little Prissy and Mama took turns looking after Rosie and Mabel. What a strange situation. Prissy felt sorry for Rosie and would do almost anything to make her feel better. On the other hand, Rosie never gave Prissy a kind word, or any other kind.

The feeling Prissy had for Mabel ran much deeper. Prissy loved her old grannie and would miss her more than anyone else when she, herself, was sold and living "God only knows where"!

A quick repair job was done on the front of Rosie's pen, making way for the vet who arrived just as the rain increased.

"Sorry to bother you on such a wet night, Doc!" Papa said.

The vet grinned. "To tell you the truth, I was glad to get out of the house. My wife and I have been shopping for a new car. She wants a Chrysler and I want a Buick. Just as I was about to lose the argument, ---I was rescued by your phone call."

He took his time examining both of the sows. Rosie let out a howl and then whined pitifully as he located the breaks. She commenced to rock back and forth, wanting to get away.

Quicker with his needle than Wyatt Earp with a six gun, ---Bang! The sow was stuck. Almost immediately, she calmed down, becoming drowsey and soon could be handled. Papa helped set the leg and apply the cast. The cut was cleaned and dressed before the sow was injected with a solution to help with the blood loss.

"It's the first broken bone since Victoria's toe,"

Papa reported. "That was a couple of years ago. What do you think about this one, Doc? Is she gonna be O.K.?"

"Well, she's pretty weak, lost a lot of blood. Maybe. She's young and strong. Pigs are due when?" he asked.

"Between two and three weeks," Papa answered. "It's on the calendar, over there," he pointed.

"I'll look in on her, in a couple of days. We'll see," he said.

Chapter 15.

MORE TEARS

Mama was looking after Mabel. Two lovely, fully developed pigs had been born already and were under the heat lamp. Mabel had planned on having her babies on Saturday night in the cooler part of the evening. The rain had ceased, for the time being.

"You say this sow was kicked by a burro to-night?" the vet asked as he bent down were Mama sat, on Prissy's straw.

"Yes! That cussed animal of Glenn Greystone's!" Mama answered. Nearly everybody was well versed on Piston's doings.

"Did he do all this damage?" the vet asked.

"That's right. We've got three sows and their pigs that may be half way to Portland, by now," Papa told him.

"Were you folks out here when it happened?"

107

The vet asked them, as he watched Mama place pig number three under the heat lamp. "Where's the burro? How did you find out?" The doctor was curious.

Papa looked at Mama. He had learned to live with the fact that Mama and Prissy could communicate. The way they passed news and information back and forth was Greek to him. How could he explain it to an outsider? Mama saved him from his unpleasant situation.

"We weren't in the barn," Mama told the vet, "but a young lady who lives here with us was in the barn and saw it all." Mama didn't tell him that the young lady was a hog. Papa was relieved.

"Well, if that little sow makes it," the veterinarian commented, as he pointed a thumb over his shoulder at Rosie, "she can thank that young lady for being here."

Mama smiled. She looked up at Tom Cat who sat above them in the rafters. It was good to have him back.

For a moment at least, things were calm and quiet. Tom Cat thought of Leeza and wondered where she was and what she was doing. His thoughts then turned to the warning, 'Get back to the farm before the storm'! How did Priscilla and Hotsie know, and how did he get to where they were, he had asked himself, over and over.

But enough of that. There was something else to

think about. He could not be bothered with the dead, but with the living and the problems at hand. Of course T.C. was pleased that he had been with Prissy during the storm. He was glad he had been instructed to return to the farm. Maybe just knowing the best path to the house, during the storm, had been his part in the scheme of things. However, he would think about that later. Time could be running out. The rumor about Prissy being sold could possibly be true, he told himself. Somehow, someway, he'd find a way to prevent it.

Mama and Papa stood in the doorway listening to what their trusted veterinarian had to say about Mabel. The news was not favorable.

"There's no way to stop that hemorrhaging! Her wound is much different from the cut on the other sow's neck. There, I could see exactly what I was doing. But the damage to this old sow can't be seen. First, there's broken ribs, quite a few and very painful to her. They've likely punctured blood vessels and vital organs. I can't explain what's keeping her alive. There's not much we can do for her."

When he had gone, Papa and Mama went in to be with Mabel. Prissy was close by.

"I'll stay with her," Mama said. Papa gave Mabel a gentle pat on the side and then walked away to help Will Harper. Papa and Mama were sad and troubled and angry, all at the same time.

Now, there were six pigs under the heat lamp. The next three babies were born dead. One was badly bruised. One was bruised and bleeding. The other one was just dead.

Prissy came in to talk to Mabel and try to comfort her.

"Your babies are beautiful, Mabel." Prissy watched closely as the old sow tried to answer.

At first she spoke clearly but quietly, and then her voice trailed off to pitiful muffled whines. Her large frame shook with agony.

"What is she saying, Prissy?" Mama cried, "I can't bear to see her suffer so!"

" 'The burro didn't mean any harm', that's what she's saying. Can you beat that? She's lying there in great pain and she only feels sympathy for the scoundrel who did this to her." Prissy told Mama.

Again the sow spoke. But this time Prissy could not make out her words. Two more pigs were born alive and looking healthy. Another was born bruised and dead. That made twelve, eight living. Mabel called to her babies. A small gate opened upward near the floor of the heat lamp area, so the pigs could go to their mother. Healthy pigs are born with their eyes wide open and walking and talking. It takes a child two years to learn these things.

Mama was glad to see the pigs nursing. How Mabel managed, they didn't know, but she was hanging on to life.

"Prissy," Mabel called, in a clear whisper, "Don't forget me, child."

"Please don't say that, Mabel ---you're scaring me," Prissy cried.

Mama called for Papa to come. The nursing pigs suddenly became restless, as if they sensed that something had gone wrong. Papa knelt down by the old sow's head.

"She's dead, Mama," he said. The two of them picked up the babies and gently placed them back under the heat lamp. Prissy watched and wept. Mama cried and so did Papa. Mabel was loved, a lot.

Prissy's heart was heavy. "Why do the ones I love, die?" She asked herself.

"Mama, if she had died before her pigs were born, would they have died too?" She blubbered.

Mama told her, "Yes, they would."

"So Mabel hung on until all her babies had been born. Wasn't she brave, Mama? But what will happen to them now? Will they die too?" Prissy burst into tears. "Almost everybody I love, dies!"

Mama hugged Little Prissy tight. "No, darling, we won't let them! We've got a goodly supply of baby bottles. They'll get fed, just like your mother did. And, they'll grow up to be strong, healthy hogs, like you."

"All eight of them?" Prissy cried.

"All eight of them." Mama assured her. "You know my McDade granddaughters, Christina and Sara, ---on week-ends they can help. They'll love it."

Mabel appeared to be sleeping, lying there, but Prissy knew better. From high in the rafters, T.C. wept in silence as his sad little friend covered her grandmother with straw, awaiting her burial.

"Good-bye." Prissy cried herself to sleep.

Chapter 16.

LIFE GOES ON

orning dawned clear and cool. It would be a busy day, with much to be done before life at the hog farm could return to normal. First, the scattered pigs must be found.

At seven a.m., Papa went out to the pasture between the barn and the timber. He banged on a metal feed bucket with a stick. It didn't take much banging until Rachel, Carlotta, Peaches and all their pigs came running out of the timber. The feed troughs in their newly repaired pens had been filled. This morning they were getting something extra, about a dozen apples for each family. Papa thought they deserved special treatment because of being chased out of their own home on such a bad night. All the hogs beat him back to the barn. He hurried in and closed their gates behind them.

By nine o'clock, Mabel was properly buried in the

The cemetery. Gone but not forgotten.

timber in what had become an animal cemetery. Priscilla had been laid to rest near Hotsie. Mitzi's grave was to the left of Priscilla's. Mabel's grave was next to the little dog. A large, flattish river rock had been placed on each grave as a marker. Once in a while, during pleasant weather, Mama would walk back there with old Maggie, picking wild flowers and placing some on each grave.

It was plain to see that Rosie was feeling much better, but as yet, she had made no attempt to stand on her new cast.

Prissy had been placed in Mabel's pen, since her own quarters were occupied by the pigs. Both gates had been left open so she could go in and out as she pleased to visit with the new family. Perhaps Mama thought the gates should remain open, just in case Prissy might be required to summon them again. For the present, Prissy was content to come and go and to oversee the bottle feeding which seemed to be going along O.K.

When Peaches began talking to Prissy, Prissy could hardly believe it. Peaches talked about the storm and their adventures back under the trees.

"Didn't you get wet and muddy?" Prissy asked.

The sow laughed. "Sure we did, on the way back there. Splash loved it! Once we got under the protection of the big pine trees, it was nice, even a bit dusty. We slept there. Deer came by, surprised to see us, but they didn't stick around. Rachel's snoring scared them away, I think."

Prissy laughed. But immediately she felt ashamed. It isn't right, she told herself, to be laughing so soon after Mabel's burial. Somehow Peaches understood.

"I'm sorry about Mabel, Prissy. I know how much she meant to you. And Rosie! She's lucky to be alive and it's all because of you. If it wasn't for you going for help ---"

Prissy interrupted. "The vet helped her, not me. Rosie won't even talk to me!"

"But you went for help! Because of you, Prissy, your Mama and Papa learned about our troubles and came to rescue us. Right?"

Prissy was a little embarrassed. She was not accustomed to being paid a nice compliment.

"I guess so," she said shyly, "but Tom Cat went with me!"

Speaking of Tom Cat, there he was in Rosie's pen. It was not a social call. There was something he wanted to ask her, when she was better.

"Why don't ya stand up, hog?" he questioned, anxious to see her on her feet.

Outside of being a tad weak from loss of blood, Rosie was feeling much improved. Papa had put her feed on the floor this morning, right in front of her mouth. She ate lying down and licked up every scrap.

"I'll get up when I get ready to get up and not

until!'' Rosie snapped.

"No guts, huh?" Tom Cat teased. "You'd better get up and thank Little Prissy for going after her Mama and Papa for you.''

Rosie didn't answer. T.C. couldn't stand her company. He left her to make rounds, ending up, as usual, with Prissy.

"Your gate isn't shut! How come?"

"I'm sort of baby sitting Mabel's pigs. Did you know they spent the rest of the night, last night, in the house? Mama wanted to keep one eye on them, while she slept with the other. At least, that's what she said. They were really pleased about us coming down to the house to get them. Mama said, 'That was a kind, brave thing to do.' For a while there, I got to thinking, maybe she won't sell me after all, ---but then I remembered, I'm still Priscilla's daughter, nothing can change that!"

"Listen Porker, I want to talk to you about that," Tom Cat looked very serious. "I want you to stop worrying. I don't think your Mama would ever stand for you to be sold! I've been nosing around, listening."

"And I know what you're hearing. Everybody knows it. It's no secret!" Prissy responded.

"Maybe it's no secret, but I can't make myself believe it. Why don't you come right out and ask your Mama if they're gonna sell you? Then you'd know, one way or the other. Ask her this morning!" Tom Cat suggested.

Papa and Mama were in the barn, but they were very busy at the moment. They had the doors shut and were moving hogs around again. Pigs were squealing, putting up a real fuss about leaving their mothers. Weaning time and squealing go together. Several sows were being put out to pasture and several more were being moved in. Two of them were back in the barn for the first time since they had been taken out, ---

when they were weaned.

Rachel had been moved out and now these two young gilts were being funneled into Rachel's pen, next to Prissy.

Prissy watched. Suddenly, she realized who they were. *Finally*, she thought, some good fortune has come my way. You can't imagine how excited she got. Cedar shavings flew in all directions as she whirled happily around. T.C. scrambled for safety.

"Patsy! Penny!" she cried. "My lovely daughters!"

"It's us, mother," Patsy spoke through tears of joy.

"Are you all right, mother? You didn't get hurt last night, did you?" Penny asked thoughtfully.

"No, no! I'm just fine. I'm so happy to see you both. You've grown up so quickly! You, Patsy, look so much like my mother."

"And Penny looks like you," Patsy told her.

Mama looked on as the little family became reacquainted. At breakfast, she and Papa had talked it over. There would be a great void in Little Prissy's life now with Mabel gone. The daughters should be moved in, at once. Actually, Patsy and Penny were not old enough to moved into the farrowing barn for a few more weeks. Mabel's untimely death had altered the timing of this event. They were getting very special treatment. Prissy hoped there would not be ill

"Patsy, Penny!" she cried. *My lovely daughters!"*
feelings toward them because of it.

Out in the pasture, T.C. stopped to visit with Victoria on his way back from devouring a fat field mouse.

"Now tell me again how you heard the rumor about Prissy," he said, planting himself firmly in front of the grazing hog.

"Why? Leave it alone, cat,---you worry too much. What happens, happens," Victoria told him.

"Victoria, tell me how you heard the rumor!"
T.C. was not going anyplace until he got what he had
come for, and the sow knew it. He was a pushy cat!

"All right, if you insist, but you're wasting your
time. Rosie overheard one of the younger sows telling
Gracie that she overheard the Mr. and Mrs. talking
about it."

"That's not the way I've heard it," T.C. said. "I
heard that it was you, Victoria, who overheard the
Mr. and Mrs. talking about it!"

"Not true! A rumor is a rumor. After a while it
gets told so many ways ---" she continued to graze.

In every version of the rumor, one name is always mentioned, Tom Cat told himself: Rosie's! He
watched his old friend a second and remembered
what she had said the day of the storm. When the
wind suddenly came up, she had said that that was a
warning. She had predicted trouble. And, trouble had
come, in the form of thunder and lightning and a
frightened, four-legged troublemaker, named Piston.

Tom Cat didn't think about it very long. There
was something else to do. He had come up with a new
idea! He skedaddled.

Chapter 17.

GOOD NEWS

Little Prissy was practically talked out. She had gotten her wish. Remember how she thought it would be nice to be noticed? Well, she was getting plenty of attention, probably more than she had intended. Charlie and the sows, except for Rosie, of course, had showered her with compliments. So many, it made her feel shy and a little confused. She had become somewhat of a heroine, a star, admired for her bravery. How splendid it was that she and Mama could carry on a conversation, they said. Because of it, she had saved Rosie's life.

There had been no one special for the sows to look up to for quite a while. They liked having a special someone. Hotsie had once held a position of high esteem among them. After Hotsie, the honor went to Priscilla. And now, who would have suspected that this kind, shy, thoughtful Little Prissy had earned their respect, enough to be their newly found treasure.

Strange! Everything had turned around. All the things they had held against Prissy, such as her friendship with Mama and her intelligence, these were the things now being applauded.

She wondered how one act of kindness on a stormy night could change her station if life so completely.

Christina and Sara liked helping with the bottle feeding. A half dozen times, each pig had been named and renamed. Sara was more than fond of a little white female she'd named Crackerbelle. It followed Sara up and down the hallway as she "helloed" the hogs.

Christina's situation was different. She had not singled out one in particular, but a cute little black male, with a white band around his middle, had taken a liking to her. She called him Thunder. He liked sleeping in Christina's lap. When he wanted to be held, he rooted at her ankles until she would pick him up. In other words, he was already a spoiled and ornery little pest.

Some serious drama was about to unfold in the barn.

Patience was not one of Tom Cat's virtues. Somehow, he managed to wait until Rosie was up and around before calling on her again. The cast on her leg made her cranky and more of a hellion than ever. T.C. gracefully sprang up to the top boards of her pen. Back and forth he strutted, with no stops. What was he up to?

"Say, Rosie," he said in a fairly loud voice. "Have you heard any juicy gossip lately, ---a new rumor, perhaps? Huh? How about it?" T.C. glanced at Little Prissy to make sure she was watching. She was, along with her daughters and many others.

"I've heard your story about Prissy being sold, a buncha times and a buncha ways. Why don't you tell it to me, Rosie?" He continued to prance with his nose in the air, like a circus performer. "I'd like to hear your version."

"Who do you think you are, hanging around me, asking me stupid question? Get off my fence! You were not invited," Rosie huffed.

"Don't, Tom Cat," Prissy cried. "I know you're just trying to help, but please don't talk about it! Papa and Mama are going to sell me, no matter what you get Rosie to admit, and it's nobody's fault."

Tom Cat stopped and stared. In the front doorway stood Mama and the girls, listening! Mama looked surprised!

"What did you say, Prissy?"

"Oh, nothing!" The little sow answered shyly. "I --I didn't know you were listening."

"Prissy, darling, I heard what you said, but I can't

Mama and the girls were listening

believe you said it! Do you really think that Papa and I could ever sell you? We love you, Prissy," Mama told her, and went in to give the troubled little sow a hug.

"But Rosie told me. Someone heard you say it," Prissy cried.

"Rosie is badly mistaken! Never, could we say a thing like that!"

Prissy had been so sure for so long that the rumor might be true. Now she had heard the denial from Mama. Finally, the truth. Scrud, she thought, why didn't I ask her a long time ago? Relief came to her in the form of laughter and tears.

T.C. stood firm and spewed forth fiery words of anger. He literally convulsed with rage.

"I knew you lied, sow! How long my friend has worried and suffered because of your mouth. You made the whole thing up, didn't you? I suppose it would be asking too much for you to apologize to Prissy?"

Rosie truly appeared to be a heartless hog, for she paid very little attention to Tom Cat's ranting. Too bad, since he did it so well. Perhaps one day Rosie would have a change of heart.

"T.C.," Prissy called. "Don't let it worry you. Ask me if I care what she thinks! I don't! As long as this is my home forever, I'm content." And, she truly was.

"I'll never let Rosie forget about you saving her life." The cat put in one more lick.

Patsy and Penny took an immediate dislike to Rosie.

"How dare you treat our mother so cruelly?" Patsy shouted. "May all your apples be full of maggots!"

Not to be outdone by her sister, Penny spoke her mind, as well.

"And may your morning breakfast be full of mouse dung!"

"That wasn't very nice, Penny," Prissy giggled.

"It wasn't meant to be nice, mother," her daughter answered.

In walked Papa with a message. "Glenn Greystone and I just finished loading those two burros on a truck. Piston wasn't very happy about it. They're headed for a ranch in Montana belonging to Glenn's brother."

Mama laughed. "What a horrible thing to do to his brother."

"That is exactly what I told him," Papa said as he headed out the door. Once he was outside the barn, they heard him greet a visitor.

"Well hello! Where did you come from?" He came back in, carrying the most beautiful, blue eyed, white cat any of them had ever seen. "Would you look at this pretty thing, Mama!"

"Can we keep him here, Grandpa?" Sara asked.

"I think it's a 'her' , Sara, and yes, if she likes us and wants to stay," Papa answered.

"She's absolutely gorgeous," Mama agreed, stroking the cat's back. "If she decides to stay, she will really pretty up the place."

T.C. nearly fell off Rosie's fence! It can't be, he told himself, as he grinned his broadest grin. Quickly, he regained his composure and with one graceful lunge landed near Papa's feet.

"Leeza!" He seemed to sing her name.

Down from Papa's arms she flew. For once in his life, Tom Cat was so overjoyed that he was rendered speechless! She purred a joyful sound as she rubbed her head slowly along T.C.'s neck.

Oh, such an extraordinary cat is this Tom Cat. To think, a lovely feline such as this had followed him home.

Little Prissy could see that her friend was very happy. Come to think of it, she was pretty happy herself. And why not? Her daughters were right next

Leeza and Tom Cat

door; Mabel's pigs, all eight of them, were looking great! She had plenty of conversation and best of all, the rumor had been false. Piston, ---she hoped he would not bust up the truck too much before it got to Montana.

The little sow breathed a big sigh, straightened her straw and laid down to pleasant dreams. In two weeks she would have a new batch of pigs to care for. Maybe they wouldn't be too pesky!

"Good-bye hogs," Christina yelled as she left the barn.

"Good-bye for now, hogs," Sara echoed.

"Good-bye Crackerbelle."

"Good-bye Thunder."